THE BLACK BULL OF ARDALBA

The Publishers gratefully acknowledge the financial assistance of The Arts Council/An Chomhairle Ealaíon

First published in 2002 by Mercier Press
5 French Church Street Cork
Tel: (021) 4275040; Fax: (021) 4274969
E.mail: books@mercier.ie
www.mercier.ie

16 Hume Street Dublin 2
Tel: (01) 661 5299; Fax: (01) 661 8583
E.mail: books@marino.ie

Trade enquiries to CMD Distribution
55a Spruce Avenue
Stillorgan Industrial Park
Blackrock County Dublin
Tel: (01) 294 2560; Fax: (01) 294 2565
E.mail: cmd@columba.ie

ISBN 1 85635 385 0
10 9 8 7 6 5 4 3 2 1

A CIP record for this title is available from the British Library

Cover design by Mercier Press
Cover illustration by Oona MacFarland

Printed in Ireland by ColourBooks, Baldoyle Industrial Estate, Dublin 13

The Black Bull of Ardalba

Máire Welford

Máire Welford

I dedicate this book
to
George

CONTENTS

1

The Valley of Rocks

Aidan, Roisín, Rory and Brona stood at the entrance to the cave.

'Are we going in or not?' Roisín asked impatiently. She looked at each of her friends in turn, her dark blue eyes daring them to say no.

'I vote we do,' Brona said. 'I've even brought a torch because it was so dark last year, and I thought we might want to go into the inside cave this time.' Brona was always thinking ahead. She believed in being ready for anything. 'What do *you* think, Aidan?' she asked, turning to the tallest member of the group.

'OK by me. Maybe we will get as far as the inner cave today,' he said.

'Well, I vote we all go home.' Rory sounded cross. 'I don't like caves,' he said. 'I never did. And I didn't like this one last year.'

'I vote we go in.' Roisín's tone was definite. She tossed her long brown ponytail over her shoulder. 'That makes it three to one.' Her look challenged Rory to argue with her.

'If you don't want to come, why don't you wait for us

here?' Aidan was sounding impatient now. 'If we don't get going, the whole afternoon will be wasted.'

Rory shrugged and said nothing. They all knew he would go with them. They always went everywhere together.

The cave was in the Valley of Rocks, near its centre. The Valley of Rocks was a strange place. You could get to it by going down the road past Rory's house, or by going past the school, as they had done today. In the middle of green fields, not far from the River Whitewater and next door to Glenelk, the town where they all lived, you suddenly stepped down into a depression where nothing grew. It was bare and sandy like a desert, covered with rocks that time had formed into interesting and grotesque shapes. Wild and mysterious, this place had a prehistoric appearance. Had dinosaurs once lived here? Or left their footprints? Or their bones? It looked like the sort of place where giant lizards might have felt at home.

You would not have thought that such a place could be found within a couple of miles of Glenelk. The town was small, but always busy. All day long its main street was thronged with people. Up and down they rushed, right from Castle Gate at one end to Seven Arch Bridge at the other: talking, shouting, pushing noisy babies along in their buggies, blocking doorways when they stood to gossip. They seemed impatient to have their say, or to get to where they were going.

Roisín and the others had lived here since they were born. They went to the same school, and were all in the same class. Their neighbours thought of them as a gang because they did everything together.

'We're not a gang,' Brona would protest whenever anyone

used that word. 'In a gang someone has to be the boss. We are four different people. We just happen to be friends who like to do things together. None of us is the boss.'

It was the middle of April, the first hot and sunny day of the year. When they had met up after having their dinners and doing their homework, they had decided to explore the Valley of Rocks. They had not been there since the summer holidays.

'It won't get dark before 7.30 at the earliest, and our parents won't mind where we go as long as we stay together,' Roisín had said.

Now they stood outside the cave, and in spite of the warm sunshine, got that feeling of chilled isolation that always seized them here. The valley held its own silence, where outside sounds remained muted and retreating. Around them stood irregular rock formations. Towering over them were massive, ancient structures, waiting for imagination to interpret what they might represent. They were strange, often beautiful, resulting from action of rain or storm, owing nothing to human skill.

Brona paused now to stroke the sandpapery surface of the massive tower of stone that stood in front of the cave entrance. Smaller stones lying around it suggested demon-like animals, yet the tower itself was beautiful, its top lit up by afternoon sun.

'I bet these shapes are older than history,' she said. 'I bet they were here before the first people ever came to Ireland.' Her dark eyes had a faraway look as she thought back to the distant past.

'Really? The first people?' Rory could not imagine a time so long ago, now that he stopped to think about it.

'*People* couldn't have made them,' Roisín said. 'I read about markings on ancient stones in a book I found in the school library. People made patterns and designs on things. These have no pattern at all. They're just completely random shapes.'

'Come on,' Rory said, wanting to get it over with. 'If we're going into the cave, let's do it.'

At that, Aidan moved towards the entrance. Free-standing rocks hid the tiny opening. You could go between them into the cave and disappear into the sandy hillside, but if you didn't *know* the path was there you might not see it at all.

One by one they climbed through the hole into the cave they had explored last year. It looked exactly the same, undisturbed by other visitors. Brona shone her torch around. It was like an empty room, draped only with cobwebs.

'The second cave is over there.' She pointed to the right, to a distant corner. 'The one we didn't really explore the last time.'

They peered into dark shadows shrouding the corner, dimly lit by Brona's torch, and shivered with a mixture of dread and curiosity. What would they find there?

'Who wants to go in first?' Roisín asked. They looked at each other.

'I will,' Brona offered, blowing her heavy black fringe out of her eyes. 'I like exploring caves.'

'Be careful,' Roisín warned. 'Remember how little light gets in there. Don't fall over anything.'

Brona sat down on the ground and pushed her legs into the inner cave's opening, then slid herself forward inch by inch until she could feel her feet touching the cave floor.

Then she twisted herself around onto her tummy to push herself the rest of the way in, until she disappeared completely into the inner cave.

'Are you OK?' Roisín shouted down to her worriedly.

Brona's voice floated up, with the hollow sound of caves. 'I'm fine. It's really dim down here, but what I can see of it looks the same as last year. You can all come down.'

Roisín, Aidan and Rory wriggled into the cave then, one after the other, until they stood beside Brona and could look around the inner chamber.

They saw a low-ceilinged cavern about the size of their classroom. It continued away from them as a narrowing passage, lost in darkness. Brona shone her torch around to reveal an even, bare floor. Light from the entrance they had come through made a dim path across open space, fading ahead of them into pitch blackness. Away from that path, light diminished towards the sides of the cave, deepening into darkness in the far corners.

Rory shivered. He really did not like caves. They made him feel trapped. Aidan looked around him. 'No one knows about *this* cave,' he said. 'It's all ours.' The cave puzzled him. If other children had ever come here, they would have left something behind, like chewing gum, or chocolate wrappers, or crisp bags. But the whole space was empty, like a sitting room when all the furniture is taken out.

'It looks exactly the same as the outside cave,' Rory said. 'Can we go back now?'

No one heeded him. Aidan was moving along the line of light thrown by Brona's torch.

'We'll go back after we've had a look along that passage,' Brona promised, shining her torch into the darkness.

'There's no light at all down there, and it's too narrow. I don't want to go.' Rory sounded stubborn.

'Well, stay here then and wait for us to come back.' Aidan's patience was wearing out.

But Rory did not want to be left by himself in the dark inner cave. 'No,' he said resignedly, 'I'll go with you.'

They all followed Brona as she shone her torch into the passage, which soon became so narrow they had to go in single file. After a few yards, light from the cave behind them faded almost completely. Step by step, Brona moved forwards into silent darkness, the others following, until she found a rock wall in front of her.

'This must be the end,' she said.

'Are you sure?' Aidan asked from the back of the line. 'I can feel a draught.'

Brona shone her torch around. She saw an opening to her left, so narrow she thought they could hardly squeeze through.

'Go on,' Roisín told her. 'Just be careful.'

One by one they followed Brona around what was actually a sharp bend in the passage. When they had all squeezed around it, the way widened again, so they could move more freely.

'It's not so dark up at the far end,' Rory remarked after a few minutes.

They looked ahead. Brona switched off her torch, leaving them for a moment in pitch darkness. When their eyes got used to the blackness, they could see a dull glimmer of light far ahead of them.

'You're right, Rory,' Aidan said. 'This passage must lead back to the Valley of Rocks, back into daylight.'

'Will we keep going, and see if we can get back out that way?' Brona suggested.

'Yes, let's,' said Roisín. 'It *is* a bit creepy here.'

They all agreed on continuing the way they were going and plodded blindly on, following the beam from Brona's torch.

'*I* think there's another corner up there.' Rory was getting more interested now in what they might be about to find. 'Maybe the way out is around *that* corner. It doesn't look as if it's straight ahead, or we'd be able to see the opening already.'

Soon Rory was proved right. A further bend in the passage lay ahead. They could see it, lit by a faint golden glow. Step by step they carried on in the darkness. When they reached the bend at last and turned into the light, they saw that the passage was leading them to a circular opening, back into sunlight and normal day. The opening was shrouded in bushes and overhanging greenery.

Brona's torch was needed no longer. Rory became suddenly cheerful at the prospect of leaving the cave for more open spaces. Roisín and Aidan were curious to see where the passage had brought them. The four moved along as quickly as they could until at last they reached the opening. Then, still with Brona leading, they stepped through it into daylight.

2

Ardalba

Sunlight struck warmly on their faces after the cave's chill. Their eyes adjusted quickly to its brightness. They scanned the view before them in puzzlement. They were looking for landmarks they could recognise, but saw nothing familiar.

'Where are we?' Roisín wondered. 'Everything looks different.'

It *did* look different. They could all see that. At first they could not decide *why* it looked different.

On every side lay unbroken meadowland. There was no sign of the Valley of Rocks, where they had expected to come out. They saw no roads and heard no traffic. There were no water towers or electric pylons. All signs of urban living that they had taken for granted around Glenelk were now missing.

'Look!' Rory pointed to their right. 'What sort of place is that?'

They looked across the valley to a low hill. Halfway up this hill stood what seemed to be a ring-fort, enclosed within a tall fence of wooden stakes. Inside the fence they saw the tops of several small circular buildings roofed with thatch, built around a large white structure, which seemed to be some sort of palace. The palace and fort were the centre of bustling activity.

'Look at that!' Aidan sounded as surprised as Rory. 'Someone must be making a film. Look at the costumes.'

'Everyone looks very peculiar.' Brona sounded uncertain. 'Do you really think they are actors?'

'This whole place looks odd.' Roisín gazed around her. 'There's nowhere at all like this anywhere near Glenelk, is there?'

No one answered her. They watched people moving about outside and inside the stockade, taking in their odd clothing. Could the fort possibly be *real?*

'I vote we go across there and find out what's going on.' Aidan's curiosity was growing.

'Whatever is over there, it can't be worse than the cave.' Rory sounded curious too. 'But we'd better be careful,' he added. 'Will they think we are friends or enemies?'

'If they might think we are enemies, won't we need to be careful what we say?' Roisín sounded thoughtful. 'If they question us, any one of us can speak for all of us, but only when they feel certain they know what all of us might want them to say.'

'That's what we do anyway,' Aidan reminded her. 'We do it all the time, and it's never got us into trouble before.'

'Don't be nervous,' Rory told her. 'We won't say anything silly.'

Brona and Roisín wanted just as badly as the boys to find out the meaning of what they saw on the hillside. If it *was* real, then something very strange was going on. Somehow, they had to be in a different time and place from

Glenelk. The girls agreed with Aidan and Rory that they should all go across to the fort. Together they started to walk across the valley to the hill. There was no road for them to follow. They went in a straight line across wild grassland.

People on horseback were now arriving at the fort, and others were leaving, riding across the green meadow. When the four came nearer, they noticed many men with swords and spears moving about outside the fort as if to guard it.

When the children reached the foot of the hill on which the fortress stood, they were met by two of these guards, who stopped them. One guard was much taller than the other. They wore white tunics, belted with a *crios* woven in green wool like the ones Brona had seen men wearing on Inis Mór in the Aran Islands. Both guards were barefoot. Each of them carried a spear. The shorter guard had a tough, squashed face. The taller one was younger. His fair hair curled around his shoulders as if newly washed. The short guard's darker locks fell straight to below his ears, and looked as if the ends had been roughly chopped off.

The taller guard addressed them. As soon as he spoke, they all knew for certain that this was no pageant, but real, as real as Glenelk had been.

'I am Dian, son of Mog,' he said. 'Our mistress welcomes you to Ardalba and requests you to come to her great hall to meet her.' This greeting sounded almost friendly, but the group could see straightaway that they could not refuse what sounded like an invitation but was really an order. If they tried to hold back, these guards meant business and would conduct them there by force. It would be best for them all if it appeared they went willingly.

'Who is your mistress?' Rory challenged.

Dian laughed. 'From what strange land are you that you do not know who rules Ardalba? *She* will tell you who she is.'

The guards led the four straight up the hill to the fort, and in through a gate in the high fence which was opened to them from inside. Once through the gate, they were amazed at how large a place the fenced enclosure was. They saw several round buildings ahead, some with dry stone walls and some with walls built of wood. These all had thatched roofs that stretched up to a high central point. At the far end they could see part of two animal enclosures. Horses stood in one. The other held cows, pigs and a few sheep. Aidan looked at them approvingly, thinking that the enclosure would keep them safe from robbers and prevent them from wandering off.

In the centre of the large settlement stood the palace they had seen from across the valley, built of stone that was almost white. No wonder it had shone so brightly. Far to their right, well away from any building that fire could threaten, was a cooking area with open sides and a roof supported by wooden beams. Here steam rose from below ground level, and they could smell meat cooking.

'That's a *fulacht fia*.' Rory's whisper surprised them.

'What's a *fulacht fia*?' Brona hissed back.

'It's an ancient kind of cooking pot,' Rory told her. 'There's a pit full of water and there's a fire where they can heat stones. They throw red-hot stones into the water, and when it boils they put a joint of meat in, all wrapped up in straw. Then they throw more stones in from time to time, to keep the water boiling until the meat is cooked.'

'How do you know all that?' Aidan looked as if he didn't believe a word.

'We did a project on ancient dwellings in school last year. They said lots of these cooking pits were found in County Cork,' Rory whispered back.

Their guards led them on towards the centre of the fort. The nearer they got to the palace, the more people they met, most of whom were dressed in woollen smocks and cloaks of dark colours. These people stood amazed at the sight of the children and their strange clothing. Many followed them, pointing at their jeans and anoraks, and soon the four and their guards formed the head of an excited, chattering procession.

The children heard the same questions again and again: 'Where have they come from?' 'Who are they?' 'Who is their overlord?'

'Where on earth are we?' Brona whispered to Rory. 'This isn't funny at all.'

Then they were at the entrance to the palace itself. Their guards handed them over to household staff. These people were not dressed in dull colours or in woollen garments, unlike those they had seen outside the palace. Their clothes fell in graceful folds of silken softness, and were of fine linen in rich and varied shades.

'What kind of place is this?' Rory muttered. 'I don't think I like it here.'

'No one will harm us,' Roisín assured him. 'We'll soon know what's going on.'

Their attendants stopped them at a tall doorway, the entrance to a large hall full of people. In the centre stood a brazier of burning wood and turf, its heat warming the cool spring air, its fragrant, peaty smoke softer than incense. There was a hum of talk in the room from small groups of people standing near the fire, and from those who gathered around window seats where women sat on sills built into deep alcoves. The four saw that the narrow windows allowing light into the room held no glass.

One of their attendants, who was dressed in a white tunic such as the guards had worn, but of finer fabric, went before them into the hall. They were soon to learn that white was the distinguishing colour of Ardalba, worn by its guards and soldiers, and by household attendants. As they followed their guide, different groups in the room became aware of them and fell silent, until all those present had turned to look at them, forgetting their own business and conversation. The second attendant ushered them across the room to stand before a long table at which sat a beautiful lady. She was surrounded by several people. She was dressed in robes dyed a brilliant shade of emerald green, and wore a lot of gold jewellery. Both attendants bowed deeply to this lady.

'They are here, then?' Her strong voice held authority. 'Bring them nearer.'

The attendants moved the four forward until they almost touched the table. Standing so near to her, they could not take their eyes off the commanding woman, who was obviously mistress of the palace. Even when seated, she looked tall. Her shining hair was red-gold and fell in shimmering waves down her back. They could not take their gaze from her compelling eyes of deep violet. Her powerful glance held them until they could almost believe that only she was present, the now-silent courtiers fading from their attention.

Her fine green gown was lavishly embroidered with red-gold thread. Jewelled brooches sparkled at her shoulders. Her bodice was held fastened with clasps of gold. A jewelled belt drew the gown in at her waist. A gold tiara circled her head. In the centre of this tiara glowed a large moonstone, reflecting brilliant blues, greens and pinks in its cloudy depths.

'How far have you travelled?' she demanded in quiet, authoritative tones. 'Where is your homeland? Who is your ruler?'

Pausing a second to think what she should say, Roisín answered for the group. 'We are from Glenelk,' she said, 'just over there.' She pointed back towards the hillside, which she could see through one of the windows.

'Kneel when you speak,' hissed their tall attendant. 'And say "Majesty" when you address Maeve of the Thousand Spears, wife of Ailill, King of the West, Keeper of the Moonstone, Guardian of the Black Bull of Wisdom, Great Ruler of Ardalba, that stretches as far as Shining River.'

The children looked at one another wildly, realising what had happened. In some mysterious way, the cave passage had led them almost two thousand years back in time.

'This doesn't sound good,' Rory whispered to Brona, who poked him with her elbow to tell him to be quiet.

'I know of no Kingdom of Glenelk.' Maeve fixed her eyes more firmly on them. 'Is it near to Carraigdubh? Are you sent to spy on me for Lú, Lord of the North?'

This time Aidan answered her. 'Majesty,' he began solemnly, 'we have never heard of Lord Lú or a place called Carraigdubh. We came through a cave in that hillside.' He pointed as Roisín had done. 'Now we have no idea where we are.'

Maeve turned to a tall, fair-haired man on her right whose silken beard fell in soft curls. His face was powerful, with strong, rugged features. Over his white tunic of fine linen fell a crimson cloak, heavily embroidered in silver thread and fringed with gold. 'Ailill, my husband, how say you?' she asked. 'Do we believe their tale?' Her tone implied she did not.

Ailill's voice was musical and deep. 'Do spies work in groups of four?' he asked. 'Would they not tell more convincing lies than the explanation these have given? I believe they are *not* spies, though what they may be I cannot say.'

Maeve now addressed the man on her left, whose hair was red-gold as hers was, and whose eyes were violet. He wore no cloak, but a richly stitched jacket of moss green which reached to his knees, heavily ornamented with golden beads and fastened with gold clasps.

'What do *you* think, Magdawna? You are my second counsellor. Are they spies? Is the Black Bull of Wisdom in danger from them?'

Magdawna looked at each of the four in turn, his eyes searching their faces.

'I see no spies, Mother,' he replied, 'but my powers, and Ailill's, are not the greatest at your command. Send for your Arch-Druidess. Request Scathach to enable you to consult the Stone.'

Maeve considered this suggestion. 'If I consult the Stone now, we cannot consult it again until after the next full moon, no matter what dangers threaten this realm.'

Magdawna answered with a triumphant smile. 'The moon will be full again in three days' time,' he said, 'and Lú's army cannot reach us from their present position for at least five days, no matter how hard they march. It would be small risk to use the Stone now.'

'You are right, Magdawna. We must know for certain whether these are spies, and if they threaten us. Do you not agree, Ailill?'

'Madam, it is you who rules here. It is your Black Bull of Wisdom Lú covets, as you covet his great Brown Bull of Cooley. You must take whatever action you think proper to defend your position. The Druidess will help you to consult the Stone. Then your mind will be at rest.'

'Lú will *never* get my Black Bull,' Maeve replied fiercely, fire in her eyes, 'but the day will come when the Brown Bull of Cooley *will* be mine.'

She bowed her thanks to Ailill and Magdawna for their counsel, then paused for a moment in silent thought. Her decision made, she turned to her nearest attendant.

'Alton, please ask Arch-Druidess Scathach to attend me here without delay.'

Alton bowed deeply to his queen before leaving the hall. Maeve and her party withdrew to a window alcove, where they sat on embroidered cushions and had a private conversation while they waited.

No one paid attention now to the still-kneeling children.

'I think we're in deep trouble,' Aidan whispered.

'What do you mean?' Brona asked. 'No one has hurt us so far, and as soon as they know we aren't spies, they'll let us go.'

'That's why I think we're in trouble.' Aidan looked grim. 'I think we won't be free to go. What if they think we have magic powers, and want us to stay and help them?'

Rory looked worried at this. 'If we had to make a run for it, could we find that tiny hole in the hillside quickly enough to escape back through the cave?'

'What would happen if they followed us, and found themselves in Glenelk?' Brona looked more worried than Rory.

'When we get away, no one must see exactly where the cave entrance is.' Roisín's whisper sounded definite. 'We'll leave when things are quiet and they've all forgotten about us.'

She stopped suddenly. They could hear a strange, distant sound that was gradually growing louder and nearer. A drum? No, it was more like a bodhrán. Closer it came, and closer, until they knew it was directly outside the great hall. At last two heralds came through the entrance to the hall and stood one on each side of it. They beat their bodhráns in unison, to announce the approach of their mistress.

When all eyes were focused on the entrance, Scathach, Arch-Druidess of Ardalba, stepped into the opening. The hood of her midnight-blue cloak shadowed her face. She held a tall jewel-headed druidic staff. The emerald eyes of the snake it represented sent out flashes of green light. She swept slowly through courtiers and warriors until she stood before Maeve. Then the drumbeat ceased.

With a deep bow to her ruler, Scathach spoke. 'Majesty, in what way can I serve you? Her voice was low-pitched and strong. All who heard it felt her power.

'Mighty Druidess, Keeper of the Serpent, Mistress of the Stone!' As she spoke, Maeve bowed in her turn to Scathach. 'You know Lú threatens us and wishes to seize control of the Black Bull of Wisdom. This day these people,' Maeve pointed imperiously towards the four, 'who claim to have come out of yonder hill, were found wandering about outside my fort. They said they were travelling towards it. We do not know whether they speak honestly or whether they lie. We do not know whether they are strangers who have lost their way, or whether they come from Lú to spy for him. Not Ailill, nor Magdawna, nor even I have second sight strong enough to see through their disguises. Now I petition you to enable me to consult the Stone, that through it I may uncover the truth.'

Advancing towards Maeve, Scathach replied, her strong tones reaching all ears. 'If you would consult the Stone, Majesty, you must kneel, and empty your mind of all other thoughts.'

Maeve, assisted by Ailill, knelt on a footstool offered by Magdawna and crossed her arms in front of her. Scathach stood before her, her arms extended, her hands resting lightly on the Queen's shoulders. Her eyes focused strongly on the moonstone in Maeve's tiara. Maeve's eyelids closed slowly over her violet eyes.

'An empty mind, Majesty. See only the Stone in your thoughts.' Scathach repeated this like a mantra. 'See only the Stone. See only the Stone.' Her voice grew softer in the heavy silence of the hall. Maeve's breathing slowed until it seemed almost to cease.

Scathach kept her gaze on the moonstone. She dropped her voice almost to a whisper. 'Look in the depths where colours glint. Follow them to the heart of the Stone.'

Everyone in the hall remained still. Stillest of all were the four children. They had a good idea of what might happen to them if they were seen as spies. Suddenly, more intensely and in tones of power and authority, Scathach commanded Maeve: 'Tell us, Majesty, what it is you see. What does the Stone show you?'

Maeve replied in a dreamy, trance-like murmur. 'I see Lú with his army. They search for my bull, my Black Bull of Wisdom. They are still far away, beyond the Great Central Plain. They will not find him there. The search delays them on their march to my Kingdom. We have time to prepare defences, to guide the bull to safety.'

The Queen fell silent. Scathach remained still, her eyes fastened on the glowing depths of the stone. Again she addressed Maeve. 'Do you see an answer to your doubts about your young visitors, oh Queen? Are they or are they not spies of Lú?

Maeve's voice took up its dreamy tones once more. 'I see a place beyond the hill that stands across the valley from my fort. There is a land far away in time. I see four people not yet adult. I see a dark passage where they travel until they walk through a cave entrance into this age, and into my Kingdom, as they said they did. They are not spies. They are gifted with great power. They have come from a distant era to help us.'

Maeve fell silent once more. Scathach dropped her hands from the Queen's shoulders and looked away from the stone. Maeve opened her eyes. With her hand on Ailill's arm, she stood up and bowed to Scathach, while normal sound returned to the room.

'Thank you, Arch-Druidess,' she said.

Scathach took some steps back and bowed in turn.

'I am always here to assist you, Majesty,' she said. 'With your permission, I will now withdraw.'

She turned to leave. The bodhráns started again slowly. Their beat increased in tempo and volume. Scathach swept out of the hall behind her heralds. Those remaining heard the drumbeats grow quieter until they faded away. Scathach was gone.

3

MAEVE ASKS FOR HELP

Maeve now turned to the anxious children. She beckoned them nearer and dismissed their attendants.

'You have come from an age unborn to help me,' she said.

'Have we?' Rory's voice was almost a squeak. Brona poked him with her elbow, so he said no more.

'If you are really to help me, you need rank and authority. This I can give. Today I will confer on you the rank of High Nobles of my kingdom. With that rank you will have certain powers that will protect you in time of danger. Go now with my servants and you will receive garments appropriate to your rank. You will return here later for your conferring ceremony. Tonight I will tell you the help I most need, and how you may provide it.'

The four, now dismissed, followed Maeve's household servants to rooms already prepared for guests. Each of them had a room and their own personal attendant, who transformed them. When they were at last ready to return to the hall and met outside their rooms, they could scarcely recognise each other. They had been bathed in perfumed water. Their hair was dressed in court fashion. Roisín's long chestnut locks had been brushed until they shone, before being plaited into four strands, with a bead of gold tied to the end of each plait. Brona's black shoulder-length hair was more difficult. Ardalba women grew their hair long enough to sit on. Brona's hair was not long enough for normal court styling. Her attendant had done her best by smoothing it to her head. It was held in place with a gold embroidered band studded with beads of rose quartz. The boys had also had their hair dressed. Attendants had brought locks to curl over their foreheads, and curled the ends of Rory's hair so that it seemed fuller. Aidan and Rory wore their hair shorter than Ardalba men did, although Aidan had grown his hair to cover his ears. He thought everyone noticed how they stuck out. The truth was, no one noticed them. The boys wore leather sandals with thongs that reached as far as the knee. They had white tunics and knee-length jackets in dark green, with silver clasps instead of buttons. Over their jackets swung cloaks of deep orange.

Roisín and Brona wore long dresses that hung to their ankles. They were secured with jewelled pins at the shoulders and tied at the waist with jewelled cord. Roisín's dress was a gleaming violet and Brona's rose-pink. Over this hung cloaks of navy, fringed with gold. They were lined with violet and pink to match the girls' dresses.

'Don't we look different?' Aidan sounded amazed. 'Our parents wouldn't know us.'

Reminded of their parents, they all grew quiet. 'We'll have to find out whatever it is Queen Maeve wants us to do and get it done quickly. Then we might get back before they miss us at home.' Roisín spoke solemnly.

They agreed that this was the best thing to do. If they refused to help at all, Maeve might put guards on them again so that they would never get a chance to escape.

Conducted back to the audience hall by their attendants, they found a large group of people waiting for them. Their attendants told them almost all of Maeve's Council of High Nobles had assembled to honour them. Scathach had also returned with her retinue.

When all was ready, the children knelt on velvet cushions before Maeve, while she addressed the gathering with the question: 'Do all and each of you accept these candidates into your rank of High Nobles?'

All present answered, 'I do.'

'And do you trust them as you would each other in matters of importance to my realm?'

Again all answered, 'I do.'

Maeve stood in front of the children and looked with her compelling gaze into the eyes of each of them in turn.

'I now declare you to be High Nobles of Ardalba, and give each of you the ring which marks your rank.'

Maeve placed a gold ring on the right hand of each of them, a ring with a small moonstone, similar to the large one in her diadem.

'May these rings help you to see beyond the veil in times of danger. With them you share my own power, though, as I did, you will need assistance to exercise it.'

At that point the other High Nobles gave loud cheers of congratulations. Servants offered mead in jewelled drinking vessels so magnificent that they reminded the children of goblets they had seen in museums. The cups were made of gold and silver. The bowls were beautifully balanced on metal stems with wide bases, which had filigree-work around the edges. Most vessels had a band of filigree under the rim. Maeve and Ailill drank from one large chalice-like vessel with two handles. That cup and several others were heavily ornamented with enamel and encrusted with precious and semi-precious stones. As Nobles came to shake their hands and drink to their success, the children felt accepted and at home.

Much later, when all the celebrations were over, Maeve sent for the four. They came to her private rooms, where she had them sit on carved chairs on either side of her.

'You have heard that Lord Lú is bringing his army to attack me,' she said. 'He does not want land, or gold, or even my allegiance. What he wants is my most precious possession, the Black Bull of Wisdom.' She paused to drink from a jewelled cup.

'Why does Lú want your bull so badly, Majesty?' Rory sounded puzzled.

Maeve sighed. 'Why do *I* want his Brown Bull of Cooley?' she replied. 'I want it because I don't have it. Because if I *did* have it, I could say that my riches exceed Ailill's. I want it because it is the most magnificent bull in all the land. And Lú wants my black bull for much the same reason, and for the added reason that my bull has power to let others see what goes on in places far away, and can counsel them.'

Rory looked at Aidan and shrugged his shoulders. He could not understand why two such wealthy people should go to war over a bull. A bull was not power, but to Maeve and Lú it was a symbol of power.

'At this moment,' Maeve continued, 'my bull is being kept safe at the Fort of Datho, Lord of the East. He must be taken from there and brought far away to the western seaboard, where Lú will never seek him. My people are well known. If any of them were to travel with the bull, that alone would mark it out as mine. Lú's spies, once alerted, would follow it forever.'

At this point Maeve paused. The four thought they knew what was coming. None of them could see a safe way to refuse.

'No one outside this fort knows you.' Maeve kept her eyes on theirs. 'If you were to travel with one black bull, or with two or three of them, who would remark on it? You would not travel as High Nobles but as slaves, property of Datho, High Lord of the East, taking his new bulls to green pasture on his estate on the western shore. What say you?'

Maeve fell silent. The children looked at each other. This time Aidan voiced what they all thought.

'Majesty,' he said, 'this journey you describe may take a long time.'

'Yes,' Maeve agreed, 'it may take many days.'

'*Our* people will not know where we are,' Aidan continued. 'They expect us home before nightfall.'

'You have left one era,' Maeve explained in reassuring tones. 'When you return to it, provided you go back through the same channels that brought you here to ours, you will find that in your era no time will have passed, no matter how long you spend with us.'

Aidan looked at Roisín and the others, knowing them so well that he could tell they really wanted this adventure, wanted to help Maeve, wanted to bring the Black Bull of Wisdom to safety. He spoke again for them all.

'Majesty,' he said, 'we are honoured to be trusted with

your greatest treasure. We will take the Black Bull to safety in the west.'

Maeve smiled at him, relieved to have help from people she trusted. 'Tomorrow you will make a start. You will go first to Dara Mór, stronghold of Datho, High Lord of the East. That is where the bull now waits. Datho will set you on your way across the Great Central Plain towards the Tombs of Ancient Kings on the Great Limestone Desert, beneath the Mountain of Sleeping Bears. This is in the kingdom of Datho's brother, Cian, High Lord of the South. You will soon reach the Western Sea and Datho's estate, where the bull will remain. Then you will return to me here.'

The Queen at that point summoned her servants, commanding them to lead the newly created High Nobles to their rooms.

Roisín felt too excited to sleep. After she had said goodnight to the others, she returned to her own room and sat looking out at the moonlit countryside through her tall, narrow window.

How could they ever do what Maeve wanted, she thought, when they had no idea of how to get to Datho or to the Western Sea? There were no roads, no signposts, and not many people to ask. How would they manage?

She heard a sound at the entrance to her room. When she saw the royal prince Magdawna entering, she stood up quickly and bowed deeply to him.

'Be seated, Noble Roisín,' he said, calling her by her new title for the first time. 'Do not stand on ceremony with me. I wish to be a friend to all four of you.'

'Should I fetch the others, then?' Roisín asked, puzzled

as to why Maeve's son should come visiting at this late hour.

'No,' Magdawna replied. 'I have already looked in on all of them. They are fast asleep.'

'I'm not surprised,' Roisín told him. 'They were almost asleep when I left them.'

'And why could *you* not sleep?' Magdawna's question was gently put. Roisín decided to answer him honestly.

'Your mother thinks that because we are from a future age, we know everything,' she told him, 'but this is not so. We are to start tomorrow on a long, perilous journey, and none of us knows in which direction we should travel.'

Magdawna smiled. He pulled two wooden stools up to a low table, where he invited Roisín to sit beside him.

'That is exactly why I came,' he said, 'to show you the way.'

He pulled a small bag filled with grains of sand from a purse on the end of his beautifully worked leather belt, and scattered the grains evenly over the table. Then with his finger he began to sketch a map for Roisín in the sand.

'Here is Maeve's fort,' he said, marking it. 'You head first for Sleeping Dog Mountain, here, and travel across it. From there you go in almost a straight line to Wild Deer Lake on Shining River, where Maeve's land meets Datho's. There you will find Samhain the Silversmith, who will guide you the rest of the way to Datho's Fort.'

Magdawna had his map marked out on the table now. He made Roisín repeat the directions. Then he brushed up the sand with his hand and managed to pour most of it back into its little bag, to be returned to his purse.

'Thank you, Noble Magdawna,' Roisín said. 'Now I know the way we should go.'

'I look forward to meeting all of you when you return,' Magdawna said. With that, he bowed to Roisín and left the room. She felt less worried when he had gone, and sleep came to her at once.

The following morning the group found different clothes laid out for them. Brown woollen garments, rough to the touch, covered them to their knees. Over these they wore long hooded capes. There was a tall staff for each of them, and a fabric sack. There were no sandals because slaves went barefoot. The sacks held coarse bread and some cheese. They were given leather thongs so that they could hang their moonstone rings around their necks and keep them well hidden under their clothes.

Maeve sent for them before they left. 'Should you be in trouble while you travel with the bull,' she told them, 'hold his horns with your hands. You will hear him speak in your mind to counsel you. If knowledge of distant happenings would help you, or you wish to see beyond your present moment, place your left hand against the forehead of the bull and hold the moonstone in your right hand up in front of his eyes. Through him, the vision of the Stone will pass to you, as Scathach enabled it to pass to me. The bull can counsel you at any time, but when you seek help from the Stone you cannot ask again until after the next full moon.'

So that none should see them leave, or recognise them for the High Nobles they now were, Maeve had her messenger, Alton, conduct them through servants' quarters out from the back of the palace to a hidden gate – too small to need guards – in the stockade itself. Alton was also dressed in the garments of slaves. He stayed with them until they were well clear of Ardalba. Then he turned back and they were on their own.

4

The Journey to Samhain

With Alton gone and the fort closed behind them, the four felt lost and unprotected. They stared around at countryside that was completely strange to them. Not one feature of it looked familiar, yet they had to find their way unguided to the Fort of Datho.

'What do we do now?' Brona asked.

'I want to go home,' Rory grumbled. 'I don't like it here, and I don't like these clothes. They make me itch.'

'We have a job to do first,' Aidan told him. 'We promised to fetch Maeve's bull and bring it to safety by the sea.'

Roisín had been getting her bearings while they spoke.

'I think *I* know where to go,' she said. 'Magdawna came to my room last night to give me directions. He told me we should travel first to Wild Deer Lake on Shining River, where Maeve's kingdom meets Datho's. He said Samhain the Silversmith lived there in a crannóg on the lake. He is a friend to Maeve and to Datho and he will help us to reach Datho's fort at Dara Mór.' She looked around her. 'We start by going over that mountain.' She pointed to a mountain in the distance that looked like a sleeping dog, with a long back and the mountain's peak for its head.

'Right, then. Are we all agreed to head for that mountain?' Aidan sounded relieved that they had some idea of where they should go. He had done some orienteering, and was good at finding his way cross-country. 'We'll walk in as straight a line as we can, from one landmark to the next. There aren't any roads to guide us.'

They used their staffs to help them as they trudged along and carried their sacks over their shoulders. Roisín took the lead to begin with, the others following in single file. Their way led across rough, grassy meadows, sometimes through stands of trees.

'I don't miss shoes at all,' Aidan said after a while. 'I thought my feet would be in tatters by now.'

'We only need shoes in our own time, to walk around Glenelk.' Brona took a look at her own soles. 'Your feet would soon get sore on concrete and tarmac, with loose chippings everywhere.'

'If any of us do get blisters, I can do first aid.' Roisín laughed when she said this, but she was the one who always helped when any of them had cuts or grazes, and the others knew she meant it.

After that they walked almost in silence for a long time, while the sun climbed high overhead. They had set themselves one landmark after another as they walked, so as to keep themselves travelling in a direct line, as best they could. Now they decided to have a rest and eat some of their food. Their next landmark established, they turned to look back on where they had come from.

'We're too far away from it now to be able to see Ardalba at all.' Rory stood screwing up his eyes, trying to make himself see the white palace and its fort.

The others looked back too. They felt they were all alone in a green and beautiful land. They stopped under an oak tree to eat some of the food they carried, and drank from a clear stream. After a short rest, they started off again, ready to climb the mountain that looked like a sleeping dog.

At its foot they walked through heather that grew in damp, boggy ground. Soon the heather thinned. The naked mountain revealed itself to them as a giant heap of sharp-cut stones, like enormous pieces of gravel. The higher they climbed, the more they could see of the green countryside spread out beneath them, a giant carpet dappled with racing shadows of high clouds.

Later the sun disappeared behind threatening thunderheads blowing in from the west. It became suddenly cold, strong gusts of wind buffeting them in whirling eddies. They knew they would soon need shelter from the elements. They could not survive in the open on this bleak slope.

'It's going to rain buckets soon,' Brona said. The clouds grew blacker by the second and wind lashed them more strongly each moment.

'I don't like thunder and lightning.' Rory had not yet learned to make the best of things. 'We'll get soaking wet when it rains.'

'We'll find some shelter soon,' Aidan promised. 'Let's go over there, where the ground rises straight up like a wall.'

'No way we could climb that,' Roisín objected.

'No,' Aidan agreed, 'but it looks the sort of place where we might find an overhang of some kind. I've seen them in places like that before.'

They followed Aidan as he climbed towards the vertical

face of rock. It looked unpromising. They helped him to search for a sheltered nook along its sheer front. Soon the rainfall they expected reached them in great, heavy drops, which strong gusts blew into their faces. Then they saw the first flash of lightning, followed by the loudest thunderclap they had ever heard.

'That was about ten miles away,' said Roisín. 'I counted the seconds.'

'Let's go quicker,' urged Brona. 'We're in real danger now, high up on exposed ground that is running with water, and we're all soaked through. Lightning could strike any of us here.'

'There's a place here!' Aidan shouted over the wind from where he stood, well ahead of the rest of them. 'It will keep us dry, at least.'

They hurried to where Aidan was examining the rock face, and saw an opening big enough for them to crawl through. Inside, a small rock chamber opened up, dimly lit from outside. Here they were safe from lightning and from the gale that was now raging. They listened in awe to the sound of rain, teeming down outside like a monsoon.

Keeping each other warm, they sat out the storm. It did not abate until darkness covered the mountain.

'We can't find our way now without light, can we?' Rory asked. 'There's no point in trying to go on in pitch blackness.' No one argued with him about this.

'We knew the journey to Samhain would take more than one day,' Brona added. 'It will be safer to spend the night in this cave than to stay out in the open.'

While there was still enough light, they ate some more of the food they had brought with them, before curling up in their big cloaks to sleep, tired out after so much more walking in fresh air than they were used to.

The following morning, the sun shone again and the four set out once more on their journey. Guided by their landmarks, they climbed right to the top of Sleeping Dog Mountain. From there they could see a great distance in every direction. At the base of the mountain they saw a soldier on a black horse, his shield slung across his shoulders, his long, straw-coloured hair flowing free in the sunlight. His cloak was as black as his horse.

'He looks as if he might be going the way we're going.' Brona voiced what they all thought. Was he the sort of spy Maeve had feared? Had he come from Lú?

'We'll know him again if we see him. We might not be able to see his face from here, but we'd recognise his horse and his shield, wouldn't we?' Rory asked.

Straight ahead of them now lay flat water, gleaming silver in the sunlight.

'That must be Wild Deer Lake,' Roisín said. 'It's so far away that it'll take us all day at least to get there.'

Down the mountain they came, careful to find landmarks that directed them towards where they had seen the lake. The lower they came, the less they could see in the distance. They knew that they would not see the lake again until they had almost reached its shores. All day long, except for food breaks and short rests, they trudged steadily ahead.

'I don't like all this walking,' Rory complained, when they took one of their breaks in a beautiful stand of trees. 'It would be better if we had our bicycles.'

'Rory,' Roisín said, with menace in her voice, 'as long as we are in this place, I don't want to hear about another single thing that you don't like.'

'No,' Aidan agreed. 'The others in school would never believe the adventure we're having now, and all you can do is grumble and complain.'

'I don't like adventures.' Rory sounded obstinate. 'I like things to be ordinary.'

'Rory,' Brona said darkly, 'you'd better stop complaining. 'Try looking for something you *do* like. Try to make the best of things.'

Rory said no more, but even he had to admit in his heart that he was beginning to enjoy his experiences in Ardalba's exciting world.

By mid-afternoon, Aidan reckoned they were well on the way. 'Look how far behind us the mountain seems now,' he said. 'The lake can't be more than a few miles more – maybe about five or six.'

They all looked back at the mountain, far away and hazy with distance, and agreed with Aidan. They trudged on, glad to think that the first part of their journey was nearly over. Now their path lay through wooded areas, thick grass once more underfoot. Suddenly they heard voices ahead of them.

'Remember,' Roisín warned, 'we are slaves belonging to Datho. Not a word to anyone about our real identities.'

5

AT THE CRANNÓG

The four walked quietly ahead until the trees that sheltered them changed to bushes, which in turn thickened and changed to reeds. The voices they had heard were loud now, and they could hear the sound of water. Brona was in front, parting the reeds for everyone to walk through.

'I think we're there,' she said finally, before parting the last of the reeds that hid them.

They were on a river bank, right at the water's edge. Children played there shrilly, while their mothers washed clothes in the clear, running water. When the women saw the four in their slaves' clothing, they called their children away, until all the people stood together in a tight group, staring at the newcomers. After a few moments, a tall young woman with jet-black hair that fell below her waist in two enormous plaits moved forward to speak to them.

'Who are you?' she demanded. 'And where are you from?'

This time Aidan answered for them all. 'We are slaves of Datho, Lord of the East. We are returning from a mission. We seek Samhain the Silversmith.'

The tall woman backed away when Aidan mentioned the silversmith. 'We are fisherfolk,' she told them. 'The silversmith is our master. I, Merle, will take you to him.'

They followed Merle along the river bank. The river widened until they could see a large body of water in front of them.

'Wild Deer Lake,' Merle told them. 'Soon you will see the silversmith's dwelling.'

Rounding a corner in the bank they suddenly saw it, a sturdy crannóg built on stilts made of massive tree trunks, standing well out from the shore. The stilts supported a solid platform of oak beams, which rested at its centre on a built-up, artificial island. On this platform stood a firm, circular dwelling made of wooden planks, thatched with rushes that built up to a central point. They could see smoke curling up from the pointed centre of the roof. There was a covered cooking area well away from the house itself, beside a neatly stacked supply of logs and turf for fuel.

'How do we get out there?' Brona asked.

'Where were you born?' Merle asked her scornfully. 'Don't you know you can't get to a crannóg until someone comes to bring you over to it? If you swam out, the platform of the house would be too high for you to reach. If you went by boat, guards would stop you. You'll have to wait now until one of Samhain's people brings their coracle over. They might take you back with them.'

'Great!' Rory grumbled. 'We might as well go home, then.' Brona poked him to be quiet.

'We shall wait here,' Roisín announced to Merle with dignity. 'We will meet the silversmith when the time is right.'

The four sat down to rest against a grassy bank, and ate the last of their food. Brona seemed uneasy. 'I hope Samhain has business here soon,' she said. 'Our food is gone and we can't ask these people for anything to eat. They look half-starved themselves.'

The children were warm in the evening sunshine and very sleepy after two days of walking. One by one they dozed off, and no one disturbed their sleep.

Before the sun began to set, a distant sound woke them, the echo of singing coming eerily across the lake. It was repetitive yet wild, like the slow, deliberate march of an invading army. It reminded all of them of the air of '*Óró! 'sé do bheatha 'bhaile!*', the chant the Fianna sang to keep their spirits up in battle, and to frighten their enemies. Its thudding rhythm sent shivers down their spines.

The four got up to see what was going on. They saw an oval, leather-covered boat heading towards them from the crannóg. Perhaps the measured beat of the music was to help its rowers to pull in unison.

'That might be Samhain,' Roisín said. 'We'll see when they come closer.'

In orange rays of sunset they soon saw the crannóg's master in the boat. His polished bronze shield reflected in its great circle the dying sun's light. He held his sword between his knees, large hands clasped about its jewelled hilt. He wore decorated bands of silver on his forearms. When the boat drew nearer, they could see a massive silver clasp on the belt that drew in his linen tunic. Around his shoulders hung a heavy cloak of bearskin.

'He looks important,' Brona's voice was almost a whisper.

'He *is* important.' Aidan answered. 'He's a master craftsman, and he rules over the fisherfolk.'

'I like him,' Rory added. 'He looks cool.'

The other three stared in amazement at Rory. There was

something Rory liked at last. They had to agree with him. Samhain certainly looked magnificent.

By now the coracle was near to the shore. They went to meet it and to watch it land.

Samhain stepped out into shallow water and walked to dry land. His sandals gleamed wetly on his sturdy legs. They could see now what a tall man he was, and could sense the personal authority that made him master. A couple of the fisherfolk took charge of his coracle. His slave carried his spear and great bronze shield behind him.

The children stayed where they were. They watched the leader of the fisherfolk go to greet his master.

'I came to hunt boar,' Samhain told him. 'Can you have a party ready to come with me tomorrow?'

'Yes, Master, we can,' the man answered, 'but first, there are four slaves here from Datho, Lord of the East. They have lost their way and seek your help. Also, we have heard that Lú's spies are in this area, and that his army, though still distant from us, is on the move.'

'That is bad,' Samhain replied. 'You must stay watchful, and report any strangers to me. Now, bring Datho's slaves to my camp.'

Samhain went to where his attendants were preparing the ground where he would spend the night. The four were brought to him there. They stood before him, trying to look humble and over-awed, as slaves might. Roisín decided that, without making any mention of their real mission, they should be as truthful as possible.

'You say you belong to Datho,' Samhain said, after staring at them in silence for several minutes. 'What do you want from me?'

'We strayed from our path in the storm, Master,' Roisín told him. 'Now we are uncertain of our way and we appeal to you for your help and protection. So far, we have seen few people on our journey. We will encounter many as we get nearer to Datho's fort, and we may be in danger from Lú and his spies.'

'I am no warrior to provide protection.' Samhain shook his head impatiently as he spoke. 'But you are lucky. Tomorrow I hunt. Then there will be feasting in my crannóg. When I am ready, I travel to Datho's stronghold myself, bringing silver vessels, sword-hilts and an ornamented collar. Of them all, the bowl I call Datho's bowl is the most valuable and could not be replaced. It is heavy with the silver I used to shape it, and is truly my masterpiece, displaying all my skills. No matter how long I live, I will never make anything to surpass it. These things Datho requested me to make for him and I would trust no one except myself to deliver my masterpieces. You are welcome to travel with me. That way you will be safe.'

'Thank you, Master.' This time Brona spoke for them all.

'Until we get to Datho, you can share the work of my slaves,' Samhain continued. 'You will do whatever needs to be done, as they do.'

The four were delighted they would have a protector for the journey, and that they would no longer have to worry about whether they were going in the right direction.

'We are pleased to serve you, Master,' Aidan told Samhain. 'Datho will reward your care of us.'

Now they were to live as part of the crannóg household. The following day, Samhain's hunting trip led them into deeply wooded country. They formed a line with his slaves, beating the undergrowth to drive wild boar towards Samhain. After many hours, only one boar was found. What a mad creature it looked, its red eyes glaring, its huge tusks raised for attack!

Behind the boar, the slaves chased and shouted, directing it through trees to open meadows, where Samhain waited. Aidan was nearest of all to the maddened animal when it reached open ground. He saw Samhain charge towards his prey in mighty strides. Then he saw the silversmith trip and fall headlong to the ground.

'Distract the boar!' Aidan shouted to the other slaves around him, but they held back in fear. Then he began to run with the boar himself, yelling madly, glad of his speed, which he had built up in so many football practices at home. The boar became confused and slowed down. Aidan was near enough to strike him on the side with his staff, forcing him to change direction away from the silversmith. Meanwhile, Samhain had struggled up off the ground and had a firm hold of his spear once more.

'Stand back!' he yelled at Aidan. 'Leave him to me now.'

Aidan stopped chasing and striking the boar, which turned once again to charge Samhain. This time the master was ready. He stood in the path of the enraged animal with spear raised. As the boar charged him, he thrust the spear deeply through its eye and into its brain. The great tusked creature fell dead at his feet.

The hunting party quickly came together to prepare the boar for their return to the crannóg. They cut a strong, straight bough from a nearby tree. They tied the animal to this by its feet, so that two men could carry the pole with the boar hanging from it back to the village of the fisherfolk. While they marched back, they sang hunting songs to celebrate their success.

On the way, Samhain sent for Aidan. 'Thank you for your brave act,' he told him. 'My own people would have left me to be gored. Before we part, I shall reward you.'

'You owe me nothing, Master,' Aidan replied. 'It is we who are in debt to you for trusting us and for your protection.'

Once they were back at the village, the boar was put into the coracle, to be taken to the crannóg. There it had to be pulled up from the boat by household slaves – not an easy job, because of its weight. Samhain and the slaves, including the four children, climbed up to the crannóg on a rope ladder. The four could see how secure the crannóg was, and how no one could get in without help from those already there. It was as good as a fortress.

Samhain called the four, whom he still thought were Datho's slaves, to come with him round to the back of the dwelling, to where he kept his safe.

'To reward you for your service to me,' he said, 'I will now let you see Datho's bowl. Truly, I have made nothing more magnificent.'

Samhain's safe was a great, wooden chest bolted to the platform of the crannóg, with a heavy bronze lid chained to it. When he lifted this up, they could see several items wrapped separately in animal skins.

'I wrap them like that to save them from getting scratched,' he explained to the children. Then he lifted the largest piece from the strongbox, unwrapped it, and held it up for them to see.

For a moment they were speechless. They had never seen anything so beautiful. The bowl was wide. Aidan placed his forearm across its widest part. It stretched from his elbow to his fingertips. The silver around the rim was as thick as his thumb. From a round base, the metal had been beaten and worked into a three-sided shape, each corner of which was softly rounded. The bowl was completely plain. No filigree or embellishment adorned it. Its smooth surface gleamed with a high polish. All its beauty rested in its shape and proportions, and in the craftsmanship it displayed.

It was Rory who broke the silence.

'It is splendid, Samhain,' he said. 'It really *is* fit for a king.'

Rory understood craftsmanship. He was a keen woodworker and knew how difficult perfection was to attain. He could only imagine how hard it would have been for the silversmith to produce this flawless piece with the tools at his disposal.

The others thanked Samhain for letting them see Datho's bowl. Then the four of them left to help prepare a feast. The boar was skinned and cleaned, then hung on a spit over a lively fire that had been lit on the flagstones in the cooking shelter. Soon the delicious smell of roasting boar wafted all over the crannóg. When it was their turn, Aidan and Rory turned the spit. Roisín and Brona prepared vegetables. Others cleared the dwelling so that everyone could sit around inside it for the feast itself.

And what a feast it was! The children had never seen anyone eat such large amounts of food as those present that night. Samhain's steward took his sword and hacked the roast boar into slices and chunks, stacking the pieces high on bronze platters. The four, with Samhain's slaves, moved around with trays of meat and vegetables until everyone's wooden dish was piled high with food. Samhain ordered mead to be served with the food. When everyone else had been served, the slaves were free to fill their own bowls, and to share the mead.

With their hunger satisfied, people grew merry on mead. The central brazier was again filled with wood, and the light of the fire formed flickering shadows around the walls. Then singing and storytelling began and continued after the rushes were lit until far into the night, to the sound of harp and bodhrán.

After such a feast, and after mead they were not used to, the children fell asleep where they sat, huddled on the fringes of the company. Music and song continued around them until one by one each person curled up on the floor and dropped off to sleep where they were, around the remains of the fire. Even the guards slept, secure in the knowledge that enemies could not surprise the crannóg.

6

Datho's Bowl

Brona, excited by the events of the day and by the music and storytelling, did not sleep as heavily as the rest. Of the four children, she had the deepest sense of the magical atmosphere of this Celtic world they had entered. She felt that she belonged here, that she was part of it. While the others slept, she woke in the darkness and listened to the small sounds of the crannóg. Water lapped gently against supporting logs, and timbers creaked and cracked as they expanded or contracted. Outside, infrequent calls of night birds disturbed the silence. Faraway wolves howled their song to the night. Soon, in the crannóg's security, she slept once more.

In the pre-dawn half-light, Brona woke again. Strange noises had disturbed her this time. What was that splashing that had woken her? Or that bump she had felt through the floor? She got up and felt her way around other sleepers towards the entrance. Outside, the sky was brightening in the east. The lake and shore looked colourless in the grey light, but it was bright enough for her to see a raft being paddled away from the crannóg towards the river, heading for a point on the bank well clear of the village.

Something was wrong, Brona knew that. She hurried back inside the house to where Samhain slept, and gently shook his shoulder to wake him.

'Master,' she whispered, 'come outside quickly. There's a raft that shouldn't be there. Come and look.'

Samhain rose at once and followed her outside. He saw the raft making its slow way to shore, then he followed wet footprints on the crannóg's platform around to the back of the dwelling.

'My strongbox!' he roared. 'It's open. They've stolen Datho's bowl.'

The crannóg people were nearly all up now, and the men came out to help Samhain. Brona ran around the house herself to see the strongbox. There it was, fastened to the platform, its bronze lid off, its contents revealed. The silver items Datho had ordered from Samhain remained there, some still wrapped in protective animal skins. But the great bowl, Samhain's masterpiece, was missing.

'Get the boat!' the silversmith shouted. 'They won't get away with this.'

In a few minutes, Samhain was in the boat with his sword, spear and shield, as they had first seen him. He looked up at the four. 'Come along, all of you,' he called. 'If I fail to get the bowl back, you can testify to your master, Datho, that I did my best.'

Samhain's slaves rowed the coracle as fast as they could. He sat, stiff with anger, in the back.

'I know who did this,' he fumed. 'These thieves have been sent by Lú's silversmith. He wants to study my work and steal my secret processes. It wouldn't surprise me if he was with them himself. I can't go to Datho without this bowl.'

They all saw the raft reach land. The thieves ran off through the reeds and bushes, one of them weighed down with the bowl.

'He won't run far with that,' Samhain said grimly. 'That bowl is heavy.'

Then they were on the shore themselves. There was no sign now of the men they were following, but they had seen them set off and knew the direction in which they went. Samhain put his slaves in the order he wanted them to travel, with two beside him and the rest following. He placed the four children at the back of the line.

'I don't want any of you hurt,' he said. 'Datho might expect me to give him slaves in place of you. And now I owe two of you for your help. The best way I can repay you is to keep you safe.'

The party set out to pursue the thieves. For the four, it was another day of hard travel they were not used to. They trudged on in silence, glad of brief rest stops when Samhain thought of it.

'This isn't getting us any nearer to the Black Bull,' Aidan said, when Samhain's people were too far off to hear. 'I hope Lú won't get to it first.'

'Of course he won't,' Roisín replied confidently. 'For a start, he doesn't know where it is. And he doesn't know about us.'

'Can we be sure of that?' Rory asked. 'He seems to have a pretty good spy network. How do we know whether or not he has had us followed?'

'We've met so few people since we left Ardalba. Surely we'd have noticed if one of them was a spy.' What Brona said sounded sensible, but Aidan was not satisfied.

'That's the whole point of spies,' he said. 'If they *are* good, no one notices them.'

'What can we do, anyway?' Roisín asked. 'We have to stay with Samhain. We have no chance of getting to Datho's fort without him.' So they continued to follow the silversmith until late afternoon, when they found themselves on the edge of a thick wood.

'Here's where we spread out,' Samhain told everybody. He lined up his people side by side to do a search of the area. This time he included the four, putting them on the end of the line.

'Stay in sight of the person beside you,' he told all of them. 'Move forward step by step, and silently. They won't expect us to have followed so far. They will assume we did not know which way they headed.'

The line moved on, the slaves scanning the ground in front of them, poking leaves with their staffs, moving carefully round each tree, treading silently and not uttering a word.

The thieves had been up all night. Rory wondered if they might stop to sleep, secure in the belief that they had got away. He was on the end of the line, beside Brona, and gradually, without him noticing, the gap between them widened as he moved more towards his right. On he crept, going further away from the others without realising it. Trees thickened around him, keeping out more of the light. He could hear leaves rustle beneath his bare feet, and tried to tread more gently. He carried on in this forest hush, his eyes missing nothing.

Suddenly he saw them: three men stretched out on the ground, fast asleep. Rory stopped moving. He waited to see if anyone stirred or seemed to be waking. He turned to his left, where he should have seen Brona, but because he had veered too far to the right, he was out of touch with Samhain's entire group. For the moment he was on his own.

He wondered what he could do. He examined the sleeping men again. Their weapons lay beside them, and their shields. What was that bundle by one man's head? What would they wrap so carefully in animal skin? Then he thought, what would they have *found* wrapped in animal skin? He remembered his quick glance at Samhain's safe after the thieves had left it open. All the silver objects had been carefully packed in furs, and he recalled the care with which Samhain had rewrapped the bowl after he had shown it to the four of them the previous night.

Excitement gripped Rory. That was Datho's bowl. It had to be. And he was the one who had found it!

Rory put down his staff and began to creep towards the sleeping men. Gently, he placed one foot after the other on the ground, to avoid the slightest rustle from leaves he trod on. Nearer and nearer he came. He could hear them snoring, could hear one mutter through his dreams. Now he was almost there. When he could reach out and touch the bowl, he stopped. He knew it was heavy. Hadn't Samhain said that? He needed to be even nearer to be able to pick it up without overbalancing. He took another step, and another. Now he was close enough to pick it up without falling over.

Bending to reach the bowl brought Rory within six inches of the thief's face. He could feel the man's breath on his cheek. Carefully he slid his hands under the bowl and its animal skin, and prepared to take its weight. It *was* heavy. Holding it in that awkward position, Rory could not straighten himself up to walk away properly. Step by step, remembering to put each foot down gently so that leaves and twigs did not rustle or crack, still bent over, he stepped backwards, keeping the thieves in sight until he reached a large tree and could hide behind its substantial trunk. Now he could put the bowl down, adjust its wrapping and get a proper grip on it.

Rory folded the front of his cloak around the bowl so that some of its weight hung from his shoulders. His arms alone could not have carried it. He crept back to the point where he had lost the other searchers and began to look around for Brona.

While he had been getting the bowl back, the others had moved slowly ahead, so Brona was not where he had last seen her. Rory realised that the party would have moved on, and headed forward to catch up with the others. Hugging the heavy bowl close to him, he went as fast as he could. At last he found them. They had stopped to rest. Brona had realised that Rory was missing and told Samhain, who immediately called a halt. When Rory reached them, they had been planning how they would find him before harm befell him.

Rory staggered into the camp and went straight over to Samhain. Without a word, bursting with pride, he held out the bowl. Samhain's strong hands took it from him. 'Well done!' he said, his voice trembling with emotion. 'Now I can keep my promise to give Datho the best bowl in the land.'

Everyone was delighted to get the silver bowl back. They praised Rory and thumped him on the back. Rory was so pleased about his bravery in snatching the bowl – literally from under the nose of the robber who had it – that he felt he had grown six inches taller since morning. 'Do you know what?' he said to Aidan later on. 'I think I like being here after all.'

Samhain inspected his gleaming masterpiece to make sure it hadn't been scratched or blemished, before wrapping it more carefully to keep it from harm and giving it to his strongest attendant to guard. Then he called everyone together.

'This is not the end of it,' he told them. 'I need to know who really stole Datho's bowl, and he must be punished. So we continue to follow the robbers. Rory can now guide us to where he found them. They will not be far from that spot.'

'What will you do, Master?' Roisín did not want to get into any fighting.

'We will capture them first, if we can. If he is among them, I will mark Lú's silversmith for the thief he is. I am certain that he is behind this snatch.'

As before, Samhain placed the four at the back of the group, telling them to keep well away from any fighting that might take place. Then the march continued, following the direction Rory had described. They went as quietly as before, hoping to surprise the thieves before they could escape.

Guided by Rory, Samhain led them through the wood where the bowl had been recovered. From that point on, they quickened their pace. An hour later, as they paused to listen for sounds of the robbers, they heard bodies blundering through the bushes, making no effort to be quiet, and voices loudly blaming each other for the loss of the treasure.

'You should have tied it to you before you slept!' a rough voice was shouting. 'You practically gave it away.'

'That's Cruachan, all right,' Samhain whispered. 'I'd know his voice anywhere. Did he steal my bowl to learn my secrets, or did Lú send him? Whatever his reason, he betrayed all master craftsmen when he betrayed me.'

Samhain collected his slaves and attendants, checked they all had weapons, and prepared to make a dash to catch the thieves. Once again he warned the four to keep well away from what might happen.

Now that they had found the thieves, there was no need for silence. Samhain's party ran quickly to where they had heard voices, and there they found the three robbers, still in bitter argument. Under attack, they picked up their weapons and prepared to run for it, Samhain in loud pursuit. 'I see you, Cruachan!' he yelled. 'Come back and fight me like a man.'

Cruachan turned to face Samhain. 'This is between *us*,' Lú's silversmith said, breathing heavily. 'Let it be decided between us. Let him who draws first blood be victor.'

'Tell me first,' Samhain shouted at him, 'did Lú send you to steal my bowl, or did you steal it for yourself, so that you could copy my craftsmanship?'

'*I* stole it on my own,' Cruachan confessed. 'Lú doesn't know about it. And yes, I did want to copy it. You should take that as a compliment.'

'You have broken the craftsman's code,' Samhain growled. 'I will pay you back for myself and for all craftsmen, so that thieves will think again before stealing their work.'

Cruachan's men stood then behind him, and Samhain's party made a semi-circle behind their leader. Single combat began. Heavy swords clashed on heavy shields again and again. The warriors shouted loudly at each other in a war of nerves. Crash and slash! Slash and crash! Soon even the children, who had never seen anything like this, realised that both men were tiring. Then, with a huge shout, Samhain gave a mighty blow that forced down Cruachan's leather shield, before slashing his sword across his enemy's cheek, laying it open to the bone.

'Show *that* to Lú, and tell him where you got it,' Samhain said, before turning away and leaving Cruachan to the care of his men.

That ended the battle. As soon as Samhain had rested and got his strength back, they all turned to travel home to the crannóg.

On the way back the four talked about the excitement of their experiences since their pre-dawn start, and looked forward to reaching the crannóg and resting at last.

'What puzzles me,' Roisín said, 'is how the thieves got on to the crannóg's platform in the first place. It must be four feet from the water level to the platform. We had to use a rope ladder, and you can't use a rope ladder unless someone lets it down to you.'

'You're right there,' Aidan agreed. 'Even the guards weren't watching, because everyone, including Samhain, felt safe.'

They puzzled about this all the way back. When they reached the fisherfolk's village, Roisín decided to ask Samhain about it.

'I've been wondering the same thing,' he said. 'I just can't see how they managed it.'

'Maybe if I looked for their raft we might find out what

they did,' Roisín suggested. 'They must have made something to help them.'

'I'll help you look,' Rory offered. Roisín was glad to have him with her.

'If you can learn how they got to the platform, perhaps we can do something to improve defences and make the crannóg safe again.' Although his words were encouraging, the tone of Samhain's voice implied that he doubted if anything could be learned. 'But you'll be lucky if the fisherfolk haven't already found the raft and used it for fire-making.'

Instead of going with the others to the village, Roisín set off with Rory to where she thought they had seen the thieves landing their raft. They saw no sign of it, but began a careful search through rushes that had provided such good cover for the thieves. Up and down they went, poking into overhanging bushes, dividing the reeds again and again to make sure the raft was not hidden there.

Suddenly, crawling beneath a heavy overhang, Roisín saw what they had been looking for, and more besides. The raft lay well above the waterline, exactly as the thieves had left it that morning. And it *was* a curious shape. Long and narrow, it had a U-shaped piece cut from one end, and at the opposite end there was a circular indentation in the surface of the raft. Rory wondered what it meant. He could imagine how much work it must have taken to make this raft, especially with the tools available to the thieves.

They began to search carefully around the raft, and, pushing rushes out of the way, they found an odd-shaped pole. Made from a strong sapling, it had pieces of wood let into it on either side. These alternated, so that where one stuck out on one side, the next piece, a little further up, was on the other side.

'Could that have been used as a primitive ladder?' Rory asked Roisín. They decided to tell Samhain where he could find these things. Perhaps he could take them to the crannóg so that they might help him to work out what had happened.

Back at the village, they found the others about to leave in the coracle. When Samhain heard Rory's tale about the raft, he sent men to fetch it and the ladder and bring them to the crannóg after him. Then the coracle took them home for a good meal and a rest.

Samhain examined the raft later. He had his men lower him onto it with a rope ladder. From the water level, he could see the sturdy tree trunks that supported the crannóg's platform. Suddenly he realised why the U-shaped piece had been cut from the front of the raft. It was cut so that the raft could be held steady against one of these supporting tree trunks without getting swept right underneath the dwelling. Then the raft could be tied to the trunk to secure it. And he understood the sapling with the wooden handles staggered along its length. This would be held against the platform's edge with its foot supported by the indentation at the back of the raft, so that it would not be pushed outwards while a man climbed up to the platform. He knew that the man who had climbed up was Cruachan.

'Now I know what they did,' he told Roisín and Rory. 'I'll have to work out a defence against that sort of attack. Meanwhile the guards will not rest. My silver and my masterpieces must be protected.'

Samhain was indebted now to each of the four children. He thought about how he might reward them.

7

FIACHART ARRIVES

That evening, there was again feasting at the crannóg. The harper made a ballad about Samhain's great fight with Cruachan. Samhain himself told the tale of Rory's single-handed recovery of Datho's bowl. Roisín and Brona described the raft the thieves had brought to sneak up on the crannóg. After all that, and some mead, they lay down as before to sleep, this time making sure there were guards awake to watch the waters.

It was Aidan who woke in the new dawn to stealthy, scuffling sounds outside the house. What was it this time? He knew there were guards out on the platform, but had they stayed awake to protect their master and his property? He looked at the sleeping forms around him and knew that of those inside the crannóg, only he had wakened. He got up to rouse Samhain, as Brona had done the previous night.

The silversmith sat up at once in response to Aidan shaking his shoulder, and at that moment a guard appeared in the opening. Samhain gestured to him to be silent. He and Aidan went outside to see why he had come to rouse them.

'There's a man swimming below, Master,' the guard said,

leading them quietly round to the side, where the coracle was tied up to one of the supporting stilts.

Aidan saw that Roisín, Brona and Rory were following behind them now, tiptoeing to avoid making a sound. They all looked down and saw a man in the water, trying to pull himself up to the decking platform. Even if he had succeeded in pulling himself up on one of the platform supports, the overhang of the platform itself would have prevented him from going further. As it was, all he was doing was splashing about to keep himself afloat.

'Who seeks Samhain before dawn has broken?' The Master's deep voice rang out over the lake.

From below came a reply in such metallic tones that Brona shivered and all of them found themselves holding hands for courage.

'I am Fiachart, seeking Datho's stronghold. I wish to offer him my services as a warrior and champion.'

'Datho's palace is on dry land. What are you doing trying to reach my crannóg?' Samhain sounded furious.

'I need directions,' Fiachart replied. 'The fisherfolk could not help me.'

'Very well, then,' Samhain said, dropping down his rope ladder, 'enter my dwelling and we shall discuss the matter further.'

While his people were helping Fiachart out of the lake, and were setting about drying his clothes, Samhain beckoned to the group, signalling to them to follow him around to the back of the crannóg, where they might talk privately.

'Do you know this Fiachart?' he demanded. 'We get few strangers here, yet the day after your arrival my silver is stolen by Lú's silversmith, and now this man appears out of nowhere.'

Roisín answered for all of them. 'As far as we know, we have never seen him before, or heard his name,' she said.

Samhain looked at the four of them with worried eyes. 'I do not ask what your business is, or on what errand Datho sent you in the first place. All I ask is that you should think about it between you. Could Lú have an interest in having you followed? Be careful around Fiachart until we learn more about him.'

When the children were alone, they spoke in whispers.

'The only person who could be interested in our mission is Lú,' Rory said grimly. 'Could Fiachart be his spy?'

'We've no way of knowing that until we meet the Black Bull of Wisdom,' Brona answered. 'He can help us with his second sight, and we need him so that we can read our moonstones.'

'Do you remember the horseman we saw when we were on Sleeping Dog Mountain?' Aidan asked. 'He carried weapons and a shield, and was dressed all in black. I bet Fiachart has a horse, and he says he is a warrior. He must have left his things somewhere on land. Do you think he was looking for us, then?'

'If he was, then he must be Lú's spy,' Roisín said. 'Someone who knew what our job is and who we are would want to follow us only if he was spying for Lú. Maeve has no other enemies that we know of.'

'We're not sure yet that he is a spy,' Brona reminded them. 'And if he is, it's the Black Bull he wants, not us. We're OK for now.'

'We'll be setting off for Datho's fort, Dara Mór, in the morning,' Rory said. 'When we see Fiachart with his full armour, we should be able to recognise his horse and shield.

He does have straw-coloured hair like the horseman we saw. If we recognise him as the horseman from Sleeping Dog Mountain, then we have to tell Samhain at once.'

'That's what we'll do,' Aidan agreed, 'though it will be hard to explain why a spy would follow four harmless slaves.'

Roisín laughed. 'I wonder if Samhain still thinks we *are* slaves,' she said.

8

Samhain Leads to Datho

The following morning the four helped the silversmith's slaves carefully to pack the objects he had made for Datho, and loaded them into panniers that were to be strung on poles for easy carrying. They had never seen work like Samhain's. There were many heavy bowls of silver with sides the thickness of a little finger. They were in different sizes. Few were round. Some bowls were triangular in shape, with rounded angles, like Datho's bowl itself. Others were square with softened corners, still others irregular. Some were polished smooth to a gleaming shine that mirrored everything around it, while others were beaten to reveal small impact points where the silversmith's hammer had struck the metal again and again to smoothe and flatten it, and in doing so had given shape to the bowls.

Samhain had also made sword hilts, some heavy ornamented collars, and items of personal jewellery, all of which he allowed the children to look at before they were packed for loading. The jewellery fascinated Brona and Roisín more than the boys. All of them had already seen similar items worn by Maeve and the court nobles. There were shoulder brooches, bodice clasps and cloak buckles. Samhain had made ornate rings, armbands and ornamental horn combs with silver inlay. There were also strung necklaces of jet, amber, topaz and amethyst beads. So many precious items together seemed like the hoard of a successful pirate.

'These all tell us two things,' Brona said to Aidan when no one else was near enough to hear. 'Samhain is certainly a master craftsman, and Datho is a very rich ruler.'

Once the silver was safely wrapped, Samhain was ready to set off for Dara Mór. When the coracle brought them to the shore, he walked in front as leader, his shield- and spear-bearer following. After him rode Fiachart, who had collected his horse, sword and armour from where he had hidden them on shore. The four knew at once by his black clothes and black leather shield that he was the man they had seen on the mountain. They decided they would tell Samhain at the first break, as soon as Fiachart was out of earshot. Behind Fiachart came those who carried the silver vessels, which were suspended from saplings, just as the dead boar had hung after the hunt. Roisín and the others followed Samhain's slaves, and last of all came two armed guards, in case of attack from the rear.

'Is it a one-day journey to Datho's?' Rory asked the others.

'How would we know?' Roisín replied. 'We're not wasting time, but we don't know how far we have to go, do we?'

All day they plodded on behind the one in front. They got so tired that all they could see was the pair of feet they were following. Twice they stopped to rest and drink from clear streams. On the first stop Aidan told Samhain where they had last seen Fiachart.

'Be careful,' Samhain said. 'If he is following you, we don't know what he wants, do we?' He looked sharply at Aidan, but Aidan told him no more.

When the sun began to set, the children knew the journey would not be done in one day.

Towards sunset they stopped at a place that seemed familiar to Samhain, where rocks overhung their path and provided shelter. When the four examined these rocks, they found a cranny where they could sit together.

'I'm starving,' Rory said. 'When do we eat?'

At that moment, the two rearguards – who had disappeared some time before – returned to the camp with six squirrels they had caught. Samhain's slaves had brought a huge cooking pot and some bread. Another two had carried fire from the crannóg in bronze vessels. Now they got a large bonfire going and began to cook supper. In no time there was a lovely smell of squirrel stew wafting all over the camp.

While they rested, Fiachart drifted over to the four, as if by accident. 'Do slaves sit down to be waited on like masters?' he asked them.

'We are slaves of Lord Datho, not of Samhain,' Roisín told him.

'And who gives *you* the right to question us?' Aidan demanded.

'Do slaves answer back to warriors,' Fiachart asked, 'no matter whose slaves they be?'

The four did not reply to this, realising their mistake in talking back so boldly.

'We are special slaves,' Rory told him, hoping to put Fiachart off. 'We have a special job to do for someone more powerful than Datho.'

'And who could that be?' Fiachart asked slyly. 'The only person I know in this part of the land who is more powerful than Datho is Maeve of the Thousand Spears, Keeper of the Moonstone, Guardian of the Black Bull of Wisdom, Great Ruler of Ardalba and the West.'

Rory went scarlet at this listing of Maeve's titles, fearing he had by mistake let their secret out.

'Come on,' Brona said quickly, 'let us help with the food, or we will displease Samhain. The meal must be nearly ready.' The others got up and followed her to where the boiling pot simmered over the fire.

On their own again after the meal, they talked about Fiachart.

'I think he knows Maeve sent us,' Brona said, 'but he doesn't know what we are supposed to do for her. He's going to watch us all the time.'

'Tell you what,' Aidan said, 'why don't *we* watch *him*. If he really is spying on us, Datho will protect us from him when we get there.'

'How did he know where to find us?' Rory asked. 'He must have a moonstone or something, just like Maeve. If we watch him all the time, we might see if he can call on second sight, like we can.'

From then on, at all times – taking it in turn – one of the four children kept Fiachart in sight.

When darkness fell that evening, there was singing and storytelling until all were weary. Then the group settled down in their cranny to sleep, confident that Fiachart could do them no harm before morning.

At sunrise the next day, Samhain was keen to get going on the journey to Dara Mór. After a scanty breakfast, they set out in the same order as before. Today the rearguards were not snaring squirrels. The nearer they all got to Dara

Mór, the more people they met, coming and going on their own business. The guards had orders from Samhain to be prepared for attacks from robbers, lurking to take from travellers any treasure or riches they might have. The silversmith was worried in case his precious silver vessels should be snatched away again.

Aidan and the others watched Fiachart as he followed Samhain and his spear-bearer. He never once looked back at them.

Many hours after they had set off, Samhain called a halt for rest. If everyone else did not need rest, those who carried the heavy silver pieces certainly did. It was as they rested that Rory noticed Fiachart slipping gently away among the tall trees, until he was out of sight of the whole party.

'It's my turn to watch him,' Rory whispered to the others. 'I'll follow so quietly that he won't know I'm after him.'

With that, Rory, too, disappeared among the trees.

'Do you think Rory will be OK?' Roisín whispered to Aidan and Brona worriedly. 'I think I'll go after him. Then if there's trouble I can come and get both of you.'

Aidan and Brona thought this was a good idea. Soon Roisín had slipped away after Rory and they could see her no longer.

Rory had long since lost sight of Samhain's party. Fiachart moved away ahead of him, pausing now and then to glance back carefully, to ensure he was not being followed. When he thought he was far enough away from everyone, the warrior stopped under an enormous tree. He sat on the ground with his back to the tree trunk and held his sword between his knees, its point on the ground and its hilt level with his face. He seemed to be talking to his sword.

Rory crept cautiously from tree to tree, getting nearer to Fiachart all the time. Soon he was near enough to catch what he was saying.

'Noble Archeld,' Fiachart said to the hilt of his sword, 'I will soon be at Dara Mór, where I am certain I will find the Black Bull of Wisdom. The four children I followed to Samhain's crannóg are still travelling with us. I think they serve Maeve, and not Datho. And why else would Maeve have them travel to Datho if not to bring the Black Bull of Wisdom secretly to some place where Lú will not find it.'

Rory, creeping nearer, could see a ruby stone at the centre of Fiachart's hilt. It glowed dull red. Rory could hear no sound from the sword.

Fiachart spoke again. 'Noble Archeld, I *shall* watch them closely, specially after we arrive at Dara Mór. Can you tell me if they are truly slaves?'

Fiachart paused, and seemed to be listening. 'Thank you, great Archeld,' he said at last. 'I *had* heard that Maeve had created four High Nobles. If these are the four, they'll have special powers. I *will* be on my guard.' Again Fiachart listened. When he spoke again, Rory could sense anger in his voice.

'Of *course* they'll never see me use my sword to reach you, Archeld,' Fiachart said. 'I'm too careful for that.'

Fiachart's conference with Archeld seemed to be over. Rory turned and went back without a sound, so that Fiachart did not see him. He met Roisín halfway, and they fled together. They got back when Samhain was collecting his men to resume the march. Again he put the four safely towards the back of the group. While they walked, Rory reported to the others what he had seen and heard. They all considered it.

'The ruby in his sword handle must work like our moonstones do,' Aidan said, 'except that he relies on Archeld to have the second sight, where we can receive it with help from the Black Bull. We don't need Scathach at all.'

'We'll have to find out who Archeld is.' Brona looked puzzled. 'How can we do that?'

'Lord Datho will tell us when we reach him,' Roisín replied. 'Only *he* will know who we really are, and what Maeve has asked us to do. There is no one else we *can* ask.'

Samhain led them on until the day was nearly done. Suddenly they emerged from the wooded country they had been travelling through, to see Datho's magnificent fort gleaming in sunlight from low in the west. It was a huge enclosure that stood high on the hillside before them, as large as Maeve's, if not larger. The walls protected many circular dwellings that stood around one large one. As at Maeve's fort, an enclosure for livestock and a separate cooking space were also to be seen inside the fort. The main building, its walls of granite blocks sparkling with mica, was imposing enough for the children to think of it as a palace. Leading up to it was a wide road, the first they had seen since coming to Ardalba.

'Am I glad to see that stronghold,' Brona said. 'I couldn't walk another mile.'

'I liked walking,' Rory told her. 'It was much nicer than walking round Glenelk, where there's nothing but noise and cars.'

They all looked at Rory in amazement. He was still finding something to like. He was getting used to long marches and no longer pined for his bicycle. He was becoming aware of Ardalba's beautiful countryside. What a relief, they thought.

Samhain's group approached the entrance to the fort by walking along the highway, but when they reached the gates they were forced by guards to wait outside. These guards wore cloaks the colour of amber, a rich yellow tinged with brown. They wore leather sandals, bound to the knee with fringed leather thongs. Their linen tunics were a sparkling white.

Datho was expected back any moment from a visit to a neighbouring warlord. Nothing and nobody could stand in the way of his chariot. The four sat with the rest against the stockade wall, warm in the sun and very tired.

'I hope he comes soon,' Roisín said. 'If I wasn't so hungry, I'd be asleep already.'

It was cheering from the fort that told them Datho was near. Samhain had everyone stand up to form their own reception party. Far down the road that led to the fort they could see a cloud of dust moving towards them, which soon arrived near enough for them to discern the chariot and its four horses. It travelled up the hill at a headlong pace, until Datho was clearly visible standing beside his charioteer. The chariot shone with dark, polished oak. When it passed them, they saw its ivory inlay and silver-bound wheels. It was a craftsman's masterpiece.

Now that the King was inside, they were told they might enter the fort. Samhain led his people through outbuildings to the great hall, through Datho's guards, into the presence of the King himself.

Datho was not a young man. His face was strong, his brown eyes gentle, their gaze penetrating under massive dark brows. His receding hair was black, and unlike other important men they had seen so far, he wore it short. The king was also clean-shaven. He still wore his fine leather travel cloak over his jewelled tunic. Samhain made a deep bow before his ruler.

'I bring the silver vessels you ordered, Lord Datho, and my own gifts of sword-hilts and jewelled belts.' Samhain beckoned the bearers to lay what they carried at the king's feet. One by one he held up his silver bowls to present them to Datho, displaying all their shining beauty to him and his collected High Nobles. The last of the bowls was Datho's bowl, the sight of which struck the company silent while they viewed its splendour. None present had seen such perfection. It surpassed even Samhain's previous work. Last of all, the silversmith presented the box in which he displayed the magnificent jewellery the children had already seen.

'You have done well, Samhain,' the King said, 'and you will be rewarded before you leave.'

'My reward is to have pleased my Lord.' Samhain, though living far from the heart of Datho's kingdom, knew well the courtesy and manners of the mighty. 'I have also brought your slaves back,' he said. 'They lost their way near my crannóg.'

Datho looked sharply at the four. 'Thank you, Master Silversmith,' he replied. 'You have done well. I am indebted to you.'

As the banquet began, the four were sent away to the slaves' building, where all Samhain's slaves were given food. Datho's other servants began to question them.

'Where are you from?'

'We don't know you. Do you really belong to Lord Datho?'

'Where did he find you?'

They replied to all these queries by saying, 'You'd better ask Lord Datho that.' Eventually the four were left to themselves until the banquet was over.

Datho entertained his master silversmith and his High Nobles to a feast which, followed by song and story, lasted into the night. When the compound grew quiet and he was alone, he sent a messenger to bring the four children into his presence. They stood side by side in front of him.

'You are no slaves of mine,' he said to them. 'Who are you? What do you want here?'

'Lord Datho,' Roisín replied, 'we are High Nobles at Queen Maeve's court. She has sent us to you.' While speaking, she pulled out the moonstone ring, still on its leather thong around her neck, and motioned to the other three to do the same.

Datho inspected each ring, and looked searchingly at the four of them. 'Nobles you are,' he admitted. 'Now tell me why Maeve of the Thousand Spears has sent you to me as slaves.'

Brona answered this, bowing before she spoke.

'Lú approaches Ardalba,' she said. 'He seeks the Black Bull of Wisdom, who waits here under your protection. Majesty desires us to take the bull across the Central Plain towards the Tombs of Ancient Kings on the Great Limestone Desert beneath the Mountain of Sleeping Bears. From there we are to bring him to your estate on the Western Sea, where he will be safe from discovery.'

'To confuse Lú,' Rory blurted out, 'we are to take other black bulls with us. Majesty thinks this will protect the bull and ourselves, but *I* think Lú knows about us already. *I* think

Fiachart the Warrior, who met us on the way, and again at Samhain's house, already knows who we are. I'm afraid he'll follow us, to spy on us wherever we go.'

Datho looked at Rory. 'Why do you think that?' he asked.

'I followed him into the woods,' Rory told him. 'I saw him talking to someone through a shining red stone in the handle of his sword, someone he called "Noble Archeld".'

'We would like to know who Archeld is, Lord Datho,' Aidan said. 'How great a danger is he to us or to the bull?'

'Archeld knew we were really High Nobles,' Rory said, butting in again. 'He told Fiachart to keep watching us, and never to let us see him talking through his sword.'

Datho looked concerned at this information. 'Archeld is Lú's Anti-Druid,' he said. 'If he is guiding Fiachart, there may be danger for us all.'

The four looked at each other. Could they – mere visitors to this distant era – be in real danger?

'What is an Anti-Druid?' Brona wanted to know.

'As a Druid stands for goodness and uses his powers helpfully, an Anti-Druid inclines to evil and is helpful to some only to bring about harm to others. Archeld will help Fiachart and his master, Lu, in order to prevent you from doing a service for Maeve. He will try to get control of the Black Bull of Wisdom, and that will give him power over Lú himself.'

'We are far from Maeve now,' Roisín said. 'Can you help us to fulfil our mission in spite of Archeld?'

'I would wish to honour you all as the High Nobles you are,' Datho said thoughtfully. 'But the important thing is the safety of the bull, which Maeve has charged you with escorting to western pastures, beyond the power of Lú.' The king fingered his jewelled belt while he spoke. 'I can keep you safe tonight. Tomorrow you will set out with three bulls, of which one will be the Black Bull of Wisdom, to travel to my safe pastures in the west. My trusted messenger, Erla, will go with you. He will take you to the Great Central Plain, and direct you to the Tombs of Ancient Kings.'

'Thank you, Lord Datho,' Aidan said, answering for all of them. 'But what about Fiachart? Will he not follow us? We cannot defend the bull or ourselves. *We* are not warriors.'

A crafty smile crept over Datho's face. 'Tomorrow,' he promised, 'I shall declare games and contests for the champion. Fiachart will not dare to refuse what is set up in his honour. This should give you a couple of days' head start.'

Datho's house steward came then to take the 'slaves' away from the king's quarters to their lodgings, where they could get good food and a comfortable place to sleep.

9

Going West with Erla

The following morning there was great activity at Datho's fort in preparation for games and contests to honour the silversmith and Fiachart the warrior. Fiachart, with bad grace, gave orders for his armour to be polished and his horse to be groomed so that he could take part in the competitions.

Away from all the bustle and confusion, the four children ate a large breakfast of oatmeal from an enormous bronze pot. They packed bread and cheese in their travelling sacks. Then they waited for Erla. They were keen to get started, and wanted to meet the great bull about whose powers they had heard so much.

When everyone else had gone out to the front of the fort to watch the games, Erla at last came looking for them. He was dressed in slave garments, as they were, and carried a staff and a travelling sack. His black beard was trimmed to a neat point, and his black hair was tied at the back of his neck with leather cord. He was anxious for them all to leave without attracting notice.

'Hurry,' he said. 'We must get the bulls and be gone before anybody looks for us.'

Quickly they left the stockade through a gate at the back, well away from the noisy festivities. The guards had been told to supervise the games and no one noticed the group's departure. Erla led them down the hill to level ground, and then quickly towards a stand of trees. When they had worked their way through these, they found themselves in a pasture watered by a clear stream. Here, three magnificent black bulls were waiting for them.

The four stood still. None of them had ever been close to a bull before. They had thought of bulls with fear, imagining them as truculent and menacing. These bulls looked no different. They trotted up to Erla and the children, to stand before them snorting and pawing the ground. The strength, power and size of the three bulls together seemed tremendous.

'I'm not sure we can do this.' Aidan spoke quietly, uncertainty in every word. 'Will they go where we want them to? If they don't, what can we do about it?'

'I thought you lived on a farm,' Brona said, smiling. 'Do you not keep animals on it?'

'Dairy cows only,' Aidan said. 'No bulls.'

Rory stood looking at the bulls as if he was paralysed, but he said nothing.

'Don't be afraid,' Erla told them. 'The other two bulls are almost always kept with the Black Bull of Wisdom. Think of them as a family. The Black Bull will lead them for you.'

'But which is the Bull of Wisdom?' Roisín asked. 'How will we ever know? They all look exactly the same, like triplets.'

At that, one of the bulls stepped forward and approached Brona, bending his head to place his horn in her hand. She heard his voice in her thoughts, like summer breeze among meadow grasses.

'I am the Bull of Wisdom. Do not fear. You will always know me.'

She told this to the others. They remembered what Maeve had said and were fearful of the bulls no more. They knew that the bull would always help them, and would willingly come with them to safe pastures.

Now Erla took charge, and got the bulls and their new herdsmen ready for the long journey ahead.

'My job is to take you across the Great Central Plain and show you how to continue from there to the Western Sea. We should start now and travel quickly, until we are well away from Dara Mór and are sure that Fiachart has not followed us.'

He organised them in single file as Samhain had done. He went in front to lead them, with Rory next in line. Then came the Bull of Wisdom, herded by Aidan. Next came the second bull, with Brona guiding it. Roisín came at the end of this procession with the third bull. They set off at a fast walking pace, the bulls ambling along with them, pausing now and then for a mouthful of grass and clover.

'Let's think of names for the bulls,' Rory suggested. 'We can't go on saying first or second bull all the time.'

'Let's all think for a minute,' Brona suggested, 'then we can vote on the names we like.'

They walked on, each one trying to think of what they could call the huge animals.

'I've thought of names,' Rory said. 'What about Muffalo, Huffalo, and Puffalo?'

'I've thought as well,' Roisín said. 'How about Hud, Dud, and Nud?'

'I can't think of any,' Aidan admitted. 'I give up.'

'Well, I don't give up. I've thought of great names.' Brona looked pleased with herself. 'My names are Torc, Lorc and Morc. Aren't they nice?'

Erla had listened to all of this with interest. 'I'm a stranger to all of you,' he said. 'I think I should choose the names. It would be fairer.'

The four saw that this was a good idea, and accepted Erla as judge. Erla said all the names out loud several times before deciding that Brona's were the ones he liked best. Brona then put it to the Bull of Wisdom that things would be simpler if he and the other bulls would accept the names and answer to them. If strangers came near, they would not think the bulls were in any way special when the four called them by such names. It would make the journey safer for all of them.

The bull put his horn into Brona's hand again, and again she heard his rustling voice in her thoughts.

'We will answer to those names,' he said. 'I shall be Torc. Your bull will come to you, Brona, when you call him Lorc, and Roisín's will be Morc. Try us out and you will see.'

So they put the three bulls side by side, each one looking exactly like the other two. When they called 'Torc', the Bull of Wisdom stepped forward. And when they called 'Lorc' and 'Morc', the other two stepped out in their turn. The children tried this several times, to be sure they were right.

By midday Aidan thought they were several miles away from Dara Mór. The games and contests would continue there till nightfall. Fiachart would then need sleep, and in any case he would not travel in darkness. This gave them a start of at least a day and a night on anyone trying to follow them. Fiachart now knew who they were, but he did not know exactly where they were going. Aidan supposed that Archeld, if he were half as good an Anti-Druid as Scathach was Arch-Druidess, would be able to report on their whereabouts to Fiachart at any time. On the other hand, the four – aided by Torc – also had the power to discover Fiachart's movements should he follow them, as they expected he would.

The sun shone fiercely down on them from rich blue skies without a trace of cloud. All of them, including the bulls, grew hotter and thirstier. When the sun had passed its highest point, they found themselves entering another wooded area. Here Erla decided it was time to rest, where deep shade gave relief from the sun's glare. They ate some of their food, and found a stream of pure water flowing through the trees. First they drank, then rested their tired feet in its coolness.

When Erla judged it time to move on, they collected their things together and lined up as before, the bulls resuming their places in the column. At that precise moment, they heard the distant sounds of something crashing through the undergrowth. Everyone stopped to listen. The bulls stood still, heads tilted to the noise. On it came, nearer and nearer, until they could hear snorting and grunting that told them a large animal was coming towards them.

Suddenly the menace became visible: an enormous bear exploded into the clearing where they stood, standing upright on his hind legs. He was nearest to Brona, who froze with fright and could not move. They could all hear

Erla's terrified whisper from the front. 'Don't run. He'll only chase you.'

Brona's brown eyes were locked on the bear's mean, red eyes. She could not have run even if she had tried. The bear began to come nearer to her, inch by inch. She knew what bears did. She had seen a film about it once. This one would creep nearer and nearer, and when he was near enough, he would charge. No one could save her. The bear would break their staffs like matchsticks.

Then she saw the Bull of Wisdom leaving the line to move towards the bear, the other bulls following behind him. At this moment the Bull of Wisdom looked like a fighting bull. He pawed the ground with angry thuds as he stepped slowly forward, snorting loudly. Lorc and Morc did the same. Torc stopped about six feet from the huge bear. Still standing upright, the bear seemed twice as large as the bull. Both bear and bull looked ready to fight to the death.

The Bull of Wisdom stopped scraping the ground and snorting. He stood motionless, fixing his large, calm brown eyes on the bear's small, cruel eyes, and held his gaze. Suddenly the bear gave a frustrated roar. He dropped back on to all fours and, turning his back on the bull, ran swiftly away.

Brona nearly cried with relief. Shaking all over from the shock, she stroked the bull's forehead. 'Thank you, Torc,' she said. 'Thank you for saving me.' Then she held the bull's horn to hear his voice in her mind.

'The bear will come no more,' the bull told her, 'but other dangers surround us. We must move swiftly forward, and on our way we shall meet with Elk. He is King of the Animals, and will protect us from creatures who would harm us.'

Brona told this to the others. They all thanked Torc for saving them, and rubbed the silky heads of Lorc and Morc to thank them for standing so bravely with him. Then Erla worked out which way they should be going, and they set off again.

That night they camped under a bank in the forest. The bulls stayed around them so that nothing could approach them without warning.

They set off again at sunrise, soon leaving wooded country behind them. They travelled down the mountain to lower ground, where a valley between two hills opened up before them. Through it ran a river, its waters so clear they could see trout darting through it after flies. It reminded them of the Whitewater that ran through their home town.

At their midday stop for rest, the Bull of Wisdom placed his horn in Roisín's hand, so that she could hear his thoughts.

'This is where Royal Elk lives,' he told her. 'He can advise and help you in many ways. More importantly, he can protect you.' The others were glad to hear this.

Erla was a man of his own time and was used to signs and wonders. People were in tune with nature, and magic was a part of life. The four children were beginning to accept the differences they found in this strange era. They were learning how helpless they really were in the face of the many dangers that threatened them. They felt safer to think that the King of Animals would protect them.

Before long they were taking the bulls through the valley, along by the side of the river. They were in open country here, without cover. At each side of them, the ground sloped up gradually, enclosing the river and the flat banks on either side of it. They felt safer here. If Fiachart was still following them, he would not be able to sneak up on them. They would see him coming from a long way off.

Later in the day, Erla and the four children became aware of a pack of wolves moving along by the river far behind them. The wolves seemed oblivious to the bulls and their human keepers, so none of the group paid them any attention. But as afternoon drew on towards evening, the wolves crept closer and closer, spreading out along the riverbank in a semi-circle as if to cut off any chance of retreat.

'I think those wolves are following us,' Rory said at last. 'They're getting nearer by the minute.'

'Not only nearer,' Aidan agreed, 'but they're coming quicker. They're catching up with us faster than they were.'

'These staffs won't save us if the wolves come too near.' Brona had not got over her fright with the bear.

Erla looked a worried man. 'There's no way we can get beyond the valley before dark,' he said. 'This is where I meant to camp for the night.'

'Let's build a semi-circle of stones around us, with the river at our back,' Roisín suggested. 'Then we can keep the wolves away by throwing stones at them if they get too near.'

'A good idea,' Erla agreed. 'We'll settle here now and collect the stones. Then we'll see what the wolves will do.'

Keeping the river behind them, they all collected stones and stacked them in a bank around them. The bulls came inside this barrier. They stayed between the wolves and the children. Feeling safer when all this was done, Erla and the four sat down to eat their ration of bread and cheese.

Soon the sun began to sink among salmon-coloured clouds in the western sky. The wolves crept closer, their eyes menacing. The pack leader decided how near they would come by sitting down in front of the rest of the pack. The remaining seven formed a semi-circle behind him, waiting for night to fall.

The blue sky darkened to indigo and a pale moon rose in the east. The pack leader began to howl. Soon all the wolves were howling, sometimes together, sometimes one or two at a time. The children sat near Erla and shivered with fear. The bulls stayed with them, within the ring of stones.

Rory's voice reached above the howling for everyone to hear. 'I don't like wolves,' he said. 'I really don't.' This time the others could forgive him. They didn't like wolves either.

It was still not fully dark. The end of the golden sunlight shone bright from behind low-lying hills in the west, while dark skies advanced from the east. They all dreaded the moment when daylight would leave them.

Suddenly Roisín pointed across to high ground that rose in front of them from the riverbed. High on top of the bank, lordly and imposing in the failing light, stood Elk. The Bull of Wisdom and his two companions knelt on their forelegs on the gravelled riverbank to honour the King of Animals. The children and Erla instinctively stood up to face their visitor. The wolves continued their howling chorus.

Elk stood without moving, gazing at the scene below him. Then his power began to change it. One by one, the wolves became aware of his presence. One by one, ceasing their howling, they turned to face him, until only the pack leader's voice could still be heard. Then he, too, glanced behind him and became silent. Elk had made no sound, had not moved. The children and Erla watched, amazed, as the wolf leader turned to his pack and began to lead them slowly away, back in the direction they had come from. They started with a slow retreat. Soon their pace quickened, until they were running. While they ran, the children could hear them, howling no more, but making whimpering sounds of distress, as beaten dogs would.

Elk stood in the evening stillness for a while longer before moving on so that they could see him no more. Then the little group left their ring of stones and arranged a place to sleep in safety.

10

Rory in Danger

The following morning the air was crisp and clear. Bright sunshine cheered them all up again, after their fright the evening before. They got ready to set off with the bulls towards the last stretch of wooded country between themselves and the Great Limestone Desert with the Tombs of Ancient Kings Maeve had mentioned.

They looked along the riverbank behind them to make sure that no wolves loitered. There, again without warning, Elk stood before them, motionless and waiting. At close range, they were aware of his great size towering over them, his antlers and noble head held high. He gazed at them calmly, while the bulls again knelt in homage.

Unafraid, Brona approached the lordly animal. 'Thank you,' she said. 'Thank you for saving us from the wolves. They frightened us and would have harmed us.'

A deep, melodious sound filled their ears. At once they all knew Elk was speaking to them.

'You are safe now,' he told them. 'In all my kingdom, which reaches to the sea, no animal will hurt you. I, too, wish the Bull of Wisdom to be protected until he reaches safe pastures.'

'Thank you,' they all said together. Aidan continued, 'It is an honour for us to be under the protection of the King of Animals.'

'Be warned,' Elk said gravely, 'I can protect you from the animals I rule, but I cannot protect you from your own kind. There are those who would harm you, harm the Bull. Be vigilant. Take no chances.'

The four children and Erla walked up to Elk then. Each of them stroked the silky fur on his forehead. Elk kept his head lowered within their reach, to greet them personally. At last, when they had all spent a moment with the great creature, he said goodbye to them, and each replied 'Goodbye' in sad tones.

Elk turned away from them, walked up the rise and continued over the top of it until he had disappeared.

'I like Elk,' Rory said when the animal had disappeared from their sight. 'I hope we will meet him again.'

Then they and the bulls continued on their way through wooded country that lay before them, knowing that no animal would threaten them. Before long, Shining River lay ahead of them. At midday, Erla called a halt for food and rest. While they rested, he prepared them to continue on their way without him.

'I can go no further with you,' he told them. 'You are across the Great Central Plain now, and I must go back to Datho. I will take you within reach of Clochan Steps, where you may cross the river, but you must cross it alone, and I must return to Dara Mór.'

With a stick, he drew a map in the dust on the ground. 'When you leave these woods,' he said, 'and have crossed the river, keep that oddly shaped mountain to your right. It is the Mountain of Sleeping Bears.'

He pointed to where its top showed naked above the trees. It was a layered mountain of limestone, huge, with nothing growing on it that they could see from where they stood. It looked like a potter's piece, half finished. You could imagine a giant potter turning it on a wheel, its rounded shape and smooth tiers betraying the pressure of his thumb. The mountain shone white in sunlight. Its immensity dazzled them.

'You will reach the Tombs of Ancient Kings before you reach the mountain,' Erla continued. 'They are on the Great Limestone Desert. You must watch for large cracks in the ground you walk on, so that none of you, including the bulls, fall into them. The closer you stay to the mountain, the fewer large cracks you will find.'

'What do we do then?' Aidan and Roisín spoke together.

'Continue along by the mountain. You will soon see the sea, the edge of mighty waters that have no other shore. The further you travel down the mountain towards the sea, the more fertile the land becomes. Lord Datho owns it all. You will find his steward in his pastures that run down to the ocean. Then the Bull will be safe, and your job will be done.'

They had all liked Erla. He had guided them well. Sadly, they bade him goodbye, and watched him walk back the way he had brought them until trees hid him from their sight.

'We're on our own again now.' Aidan said what everyone was thinking. It was up to them now, them alone, and they could not tell what dangers they might meet.

'Come on,' said Brona. 'Let's get started.'

They continued walking through the forest. After a time,

the trees thinned out, leading them to the riverbank, as Erla had told them would happen. In front of them lay Clochan Steps, great flat slabs of stone that ancient people had dragged to Shining River and laid across it.

'How could they have done that?' Rory wondered. 'No one had even discovered the wheel by then.' He tried to imagine giant rocks being pushed and pulled on logs by hordes of Stone Age men, or being dragged by men and animals pulling on primitive ropes. The rocks were so large that their weight prevented the turbulent waters of Shining River, even in winter spate, from dislodging them. The children walked across the river, leading the three bulls, and did not get as much as their feet wet.

On the far side, woodland grew down almost to the water's edge. The animals and children found themselves in forest once more. Trees grew thicker around them, the trunks bare as far up as the tops, where luxuriant foliage cut out the sunlight. Soon the children and bulls had to walk in single file again. Roisín led the way, followed by Aidan. Then came the three bulls. Behind them came Brona, with Rory coming last of all. They walked on without talking, into gloomy, forest light that made a false twilight. They could hear small animals scuffling about in the undergrowth, and birds singing high in the canopy.

Once they heard a larger animal trundling about in sparse, low bushes. Suddenly, without warning, it broke through and was on them – a full-grown boar, tusks raised, charging at them. When it was nearly upon them, it came to a sudden stop. They could see its piggy eyes glowing hotly and could almost feel its feral breath. It looked fixedly at them for a moment that seemed to last forever. Then it turned and stumbled away. When they heard its snorting and pawing going further away from them, they knew Elk had kept his promise that no animal in his kingdom would harm them.

They travelled for hours through the leafy gloom, becoming thirsty and tired. Rory began to drop further and further behind, until he could hardly see the others at all. They did not notice that he was trailing out of sight.

'This walking is tiring me out,' he thought to himself. He began to imagine he was back at Ardalba as a High Noble, with palace attendants to answer his every need, to dress him again in princely clothes and offer him the best of food and drink.

Deep in this daydream, roughly and without warning he was seized from behind. A large hand clamped over his mouth, preventing him from crying out. Rory struggled and wriggled to get free, but his captor was ten times stronger than he was. He felt himself being dragged backwards, then sideways, away from the track the four had followed through the trees. The main thought in Rory's head was, 'The others will never find me now.'

Eventually, when he had been dragged a long way from where he was captured, his captor released him and allowed him to sit on the ground. When he looked up, he saw Fiachart.

'Yes, it's me,' the champion gloated with a sneer. 'Did you think I would give up that easily?'

'What do you want?' Rory did not bother to speak politely.

'I want you,' Fiachart replied. 'I want you to tell me which of the bulls you are escorting is the Black Bull of Wisdom.'

'Well, I'm not telling you. Find out the same way you found out where we were.'

'I can find out where anyone is,' Fiachart assured him. 'What I cannot do is look into the future to see where they will go next.'

'Ha!' said Rory. 'You're not so clever then. And neither is Archeld.' He was watching Fiachart closely, and saw him start at Archeld's name. 'I hope Lú rewards his spies well,' Rory continued, 'and that he is merciful to those who fail.'

'Be careful, boy,' warned Fiachart. 'Your own tongue will slay you.' But he looked uneasy.

'If you want the Bull of Wisdom,' Rory taunted, 'you will have to take all the bulls by the horns. Then you will recognise him.'

Fiachart understood this to be the mockery it sounded like. He got up suddenly and seized Rory again, this time tying a gag across his mouth so that he could not call out. The he tied his hands and feet together, before binding him tightly to a tree trunk.

'Now you can't move until I get back,' he said. 'You are helpless until then. If I cannot learn what I need from you, I shall use you as a hostage. We'll see if your friends will deliver the bull to me in exchange for you.' Fiachart turned and left him. The only sounds Rory heard then were the sounds of nature.

He did not feel as brave as he had pretended to Fiachart. Moreover, he felt guilty, because he realised he *had* told the champion exactly what he had wanted to know – how to identify the bull. Did that make him a traitor? Would the others ever speak to him again, if they knew? Rory sighed. The real question was whether he would ever see them again. So, feeling sorry for himself, and being very tired after the day's walking, he fell asleep.

Meanwhile, the others – who were now quite far from Rory – had stopped to rest. That was when they discovered that he was no longer with them. Brona was very upset.

'He was coming along behind *me*,' she wailed. '*I* should have noticed that he was gone.'

'What we need to do now is to find him,' said Aidan. 'How on earth can we do that?'

Hearing the children's uncertainty, the Black Bull of Wisdom bent to place his horn in Aidan's hand. In his mind, Aidan could hear the bull's voice. 'To find Rory, you need the magic of the Moonstone,' he said. 'I can help you to ask for that. Do it now. My senses tell me that Rory is in danger.'

'How can we use our stones before a full moon?' Aidan asked. 'Maeve has already used hers.'

'Each stone holds its own power,' the bull replied, 'and is not affected by the others. All of you can consult your stones once before the moon is full again.'

'Let's do it,' Roisín agreed.

She placed her left hand against the bull's forehead, as Queen Maeve had instructed them, and with her right hand she held her moonstone, still on its leather thong, in front of the bull. She closed her eyes to see the moonstone in her mind. The bull gazed into the depths of the stone.

'Think only of the Stone,' he told Roisín, as Scathach had told Maeve. 'In your thoughts see only the Stone.'

Roisín felt her breathing grow slower. Then she spoke. 'I see Rory tied to a tree. He is alone. I see Fiachart a long way from Rory. He has mislaid his weapons, which he left hidden when he came to follow us. He hurries. He needs his sword, to help him to speak with Archeld. The search for it delays him.'

'Where can we find Rory?' Brona asked urgently. 'Ask the Stone to let us know please.'

With her eyes still closed and her hand on the bull, Roisín continued. 'The Bull will lead us to Rory. The Stone is now showing him but not me the place where Rory is. The Stone does not tell how long it will be before Fiachart returns to where he left Rory. Let Torc look some more. We cannot consult the Stone again until the moon changes.'

The Bull continued to scan the moonstone for several minutes. 'Follow me,' he told them then. 'I will recognise the way.'

With the bull leading, they hurried back along the path they had travelled earlier. Poor Lorc and Morc came with them without a murmur, faithful to their task of hiding the true identity of Torc. When they reached it, the children saw clearly the point where Fiachart had dragged Rory off the path and away. He had made no effort to hide his tracks. From here the bull led them through undergrowth, where brambles scratched their legs and low branches caught their faces.

Before they knew it, they were there. Rory, gagged and frightened, sat on the ground roped to a tree and bound hand and foot.

'Poor Rory,' cried Roisín, running to him. She was always the one to rush to help anyone in trouble. She and Brona tried to undo the knots to free him. Aidan took off the gag. 'Was it Fiachart?' he asked.

'Yes, it was Fiachart.' Rory's eyes filled with tears. 'I told him to hold all the bulls' horns if he wanted to know which was the Black Bull of Wisdom.'

Torc came up to Rory when he heard this, and put his

horn into Rory's hand. 'You did no harm,' he told him. 'First, Fiachart must find me. Then he can hold my horn for as long as he likes. He could know nothing unless I spoke, and to him I would be silent.'

'Really?' Rory asked, growing more cheerful. 'So I didn't give you away after all? I said it to confuse Fiachart, but then I knew that if he took me seriously, he might find out what he wanted to know.'

'It's all right, Rory,' Aidan said. 'You were very brave. None of us could have done better.'

Brona, still blaming herself for not missing Rory sooner, went up to him and held his hand. Lorc and Morc came over to him and, in sympathy, blew gently over him with their grass-scented breath.

Roisín caught Torc's other horn. 'Where is Fiachart now, Torc?' she asked.

'I see him two thousand paces away. He speaks with Archeld through his sword. We must be gone from here and be far away when he returns.'

Rory felt better when he realised that no one was blaming him as a traitor for giving Fiachart helpful information. They all knew how frightening it would be to be tied up and unable to call out for help.

'Fiachart meant to use me as a hostage,' he told them all. 'He thought you would give him Torc in exchange for me.'

'We would have found a way to get you back, no matter what,' Roisín told him, 'But stay near to us from now on and don't take chances.'

11

The Mountain of Sleeping Bears

They left the clearing where Fiachart had tied Rory to a tree and headed back to where they had left their path. Before long the forest was behind them. They could see ahead of them on their right the Mountain of Sleeping Bears. Between it and them lay the Tombs of Ancient Kings scattered over the Limestone Desert for as far as they could see. Quite near them was the largest tomb of all, a great triangular table of rock raised on rock pillars. It sloped from above their heads at one end to a couple of feet above the ground at the other. It was made to stand forever. So were the dozens of smaller tombs, which were mostly of similar design.

Roisín looked around her at the landscape. She saw the great Limestone Desert stretching out ahead, criss-crossed with cracks and crevasses. They would have to cross it in daylight.

'Remember what Erla said?' Aidan reminded her. 'The nearer we go to the mountain, the fewer large cracks we will have to cross.' So off they set towards the mountain, Roisín and Aidan still leading, followed by the bulls, with Brona and Rory bringing up the rear.

'Don't get kidnapped again,' they warned Rory. 'Keep up with the rest of us.'

Nearer the mountain, the ground was more broken. Flat slabs of limestone separated by deep cracks gave way to a desert of rough gravel where their bare feet were cut on the stones' sharp edges. The danger of stepping into fissured stone was not a problem now, but their pace slowed over this painful territory.

Soon the children realised that they did not want to be stuck out in this open countryside at nightfall. 'We'll have to find a safe place before dark,' Roisín told them.

They stopped to look carefully at the mountain which was now so close to them, hoping for some rock or overhang where they could shelter. In this bare place they needed to find somewhere to hide for themselves and the bulls, a place where they could not be seen from afar, or be crept up on as they slept. They knew that their enemies had sharp eyes, and that Fiachart had Archeld to point him in the right direction.

'Look,' Brona said after they had been searching for a while. She pointed at the mountain. 'Look, halfway up it looks broken. Could that be a cave?'

The others looked to see where she was pointing. It was a climb up from where they were standing, but they decided to go and examine it.

'We won't be any worse off up there than we are here, even if there's nothing there.' Rory sounded sensible about it.

So they set off to climb the mountain, the patient bulls following their lead. Up and up they went. The higher they got, the more beautiful the limestone looked in the golden light from the sinking sun.

When they reached the place that had caught Brona's eye, they saw it was indeed a cave. The wide opening allowed plenty of light into the chamber. The bulls could get inside without difficulty and would remain hidden from searching eyes below.

'Look there.' Aidan pointed to one side. 'This must be where bears sleep in winter.'

They saw two rounded depressions where bears could have curled up during hibernation. No wonder people called it the Mountain of Sleeping Bears.

The cave was not cold. Soon they were feeling sleepy after their long day. At that point they heard, to their horror, something or someone approaching the cave across the loose stones that covered the mountainside. They watched the entrance fearfully. Through it they saw a huge bear, outlined against the sky. He filled the opening, sitting in it and facing outward. There was no escape. Brona began to tremble. She had not forgotten the bear she had already met.

The Bull of Wisdom walked over to her and placed his horn in her hand.

'Torc says the bear has been sent by Elk to protect us,' she told the others. 'He will stay until morning.'

They felt safer then, and were soon fast asleep.

The following day they started down the mountain early, after thanking their bear guardian, who had watched over them. The Bull of Wisdom spent some time with the bear before he followed the children. Then he spoke through Rory.

'The bear saw Fiachart going past in yesterday evening's twilight. He is ahead of us now,' he told them all. 'The limestone holds no tracks of ours for him to follow. He did not see where we turned aside towards the cave. He continued on past the mountain. He will reach Datho's pastures before us, but is no longer a danger to us on our way.'

Everyone was relieved to hear this. They knew that once they reached Datho's pastures, his people would protect them.

Before long they saw blue sea in the distance. They all took heart to know they were near their journey's end, though they still had a long way to walk. Soon they were off the Limestone Desert, back among trees and grassy meadows. The further down the mountain they came, the richer the soil and the lusher the vegetation became.

Fertile grasslands soon gave way to cultivated land. In the distance they saw isolated dwellings, and on a small lake, a crannóg like Samhain's.

Now they were so near the sea they could smell its briny fragrance. While they wondered which way they should go, three armed men appeared ahead of them. These men wore blue cloaks the colour of irises over their white tunics. They had circular shields of wood and leather held to their backs with leather thongs that were strapped across their chests. They carried swords in their right hands and spears in their left. Bronze headbands circled their foreheads. Their black hair straggled down untidily from underneath the bands. They did not look like a welcoming committee.

When Aidan saw these men hurrying towards them with swords at the ready, he held the others back. 'We tell these guards nothing, except that we are looking for Datho's Steward of the West,' he said. 'Right?'

They all nodded agreement, and waited in silence.

The armed men continued to approach and eventually they stood in front of the four. 'We protect the Steward of the West and wear his colours,' the tallest one told them, touching his blue cloak. 'We know you are thieves and deceivers who wish to harm him. Come with us.'

'We are not thieves,' Brona protested. 'We bear a message for the Steward from Lord Datho, who has sent us to bring these bulls to him. Take us to the Steward at once.'

'A guest newly arrived from Datho's stronghold at Dara Mór warned us you were on your way.' The shortest guard seemed to be in command. 'You deceived Datho by claiming you had been sent by Maeve of the Thousand Spears. Then you stole his three best bulls and made off with them.'

'If that were true,' Rory answered, 'we would be foolish to bring them here to the Steward, wouldn't we?'

'We demand to meet the Steward.' Roisín spoke firmly. 'We demand to face our accuser in his presence, and be given the chance to defend ourselves.'

'That's enough,' the short guard replied. 'Be silent and come with us. Or would you prefer to be bound and dragged away?'

The children exchanged glances and shrugged. Better to go quietly than risk getting hurt. They followed two of the guards, while the third led the bulls away.

'The bulls will be safe,' Aidan whispered, so that the guards could not hear him. 'If they think we stole them from Datho, then they are still Datho's property. The Steward will allow no harm to come to them.'

'What I'd like to know,' Rory muttered, 'is where Fiachart is now. We know he went ahead of us at the Mountain of

Sleeping Bears. Could he be this newly arrived guest they say is accusing us?'

'He didn't know where we were going,' Roisín reminded them. 'That's why he followed us all the time.'

'If we were heading west, where else would we be going?' Brona suddenly worked it out. 'Datho owns the western seaboard and its pastures, stretching over many miles.'

'Who else besides Fiachart would tell lies about us, anyway? We look like slaves to everyone else, going about our master's business. Only Fiachart suspects otherwise. It *has* to be him.' Rory was sure about this.

They had reached a round, thatched hut that stood outside the fort's stockade. 'Cool your heels in there,' their guard said. 'The Steward will see you whenever he gets round to it.'

Inside, the hut was dark once the opening had been closed and secured. Some light still entered through a hole in the centre of the roof, which all these huts had instead of a chimney. The four sat around and prepared to wait. What else could they do? They could not consult the bull, and thought that without him they could not use their moonstones to find ways to help themselves.

Before dark, a slave brought them some bread and water. They knew then they would be there for the night. After such a long journey and so much excitement, they were all very tired, and slept soundly in spite of their fears.

12

Safety in the West

The following morning, before the day had warmed up, the children were brought before the Steward and the High Nobles of his household. The Steward's name was Cathba. Fair-haired and tall, like many of the Celtic people they had met, with an angry scar running from temple to chin, he wore a High Noble's ring and looked as powerful as Datho himself. His long blue cloak was lavishly embroidered all around the edge with squares and circles of gold and silver thread.

The four stood in front of him and looked him straight in the eye. Still dressed as slaves, they no longer behaved like slaves, but faced Cathba as equals. He examined them for a long moment. When he spoke, his voice was resonant and deep.

'We have ways to punish runaway slaves,' he began. 'We have penalties for cattle thieves. We can deal with deceitful pretenders. What punishment could be severe enough for people who are all three?'

Brona broke the silence that followed Cathba's words. 'We are none of these things. We bring you two bulls from Lord Datho, together with Queen Maeve's Black Bull of

Wisdom, which he wishes you to keep safely. As to accusations, let our accuser face us to make his charges in public before your household. That is our right.'

The Steward looked at them in silence while he considered his decision. 'That is indeed your right,' he agreed, 'the only right you have.'

He signalled to an attendant, who bowed and left the room. Everyone waited without a word. The four kept their eyes on the door through which Cathba's attendant would return.

In the stillness of the hall they heard footsteps approach, until at last the attendant entered, escorting Fiachart with deference.

'Ha!' Rory snorted. 'I knew it was him. It had to be.'

'Silence!' The Steward spoke the word like a whiplash. Then he turned to Fiachart. 'Noble Fiachart, I request that you state your accusations before the prisoners, here in the presence of my household. That is their right under law.'

Fiachart, looking smug, faced the four. He accused them of lying to Datho by telling him they were under orders from Maeve. He pointed out that they were living another lie – claiming to be High Nobles, yet dressing and behaving like slaves. 'You can't be both,' he said. 'So which is the lie?'

Roisín interrupted him. 'How do *you* know what we said to Lord Datho? You were not present at any interview we had with him. Maybe you found out from Archeld when you used your sword to consult him after you kidnapped Rory and tied him to a tree.'

'That's a good point,' the Steward agreed. 'How *did* you know they saw Datho privately? And how do you know what they said to him? And is it true you know that fiend Archeld, and can contact him by magic means whenever you wish?'

'You also accuse us of stealing three bulls,' Aidan reminded him. 'If you knew we were thieves and deceivers, why did you not warn Datho? Why did you let us get away without detection?'

Fiachart had no reply to this. While he was trying to think what he should say next, Brona spoke. 'Lord Steward, not only can Fiachart not prove his accusations against us, but we have counter-accusations to make against him.'

'Yes, we have,' Rory butted in, 'and I want to make them.'

He stepped away from the others to stand directly in front of the champion. 'Fiachart, I formally accuse you of being a spy of Lord Lú. I accuse you of deceiving the silversmith and Lord Datho about this. I accuse you of following us by Archeld's magic. I accuse you of kidnapping me and leaving me tied up. I accuse you of being determined to steal the Bull of Wisdom yourself, to bring it to your master Lú, Lord of the North.'

There was a startled silence in the room after Rory stopped talking. The shocked Steward asked the children if *they* could prove their accusations.

'We are truly High Nobles of Queen Maeve,' Brona told him. 'Look at our rings of rank.'

They pulled out the moonstone rings they still wore around their necks, and held them up for Cathba to see.

'Ha!' snorted Fiachart in his turn, 'I told you they stole them too.'

'Quiet, Sir,' commanded the Steward. 'Have you other proof?' he asked the four. 'The rings may prove your status as High Nobles, and therefore that you are not thieves and liars. They do not prove your accusations against Fiachart.'

Roisín bowed to Cathba. 'Please have our bulls brought in. Then we can prove what we say.'

The High Nobles and the Steward all looked around at each other, rolling their eyes, as if to say, 'These people are mad.' Whatever he thought, Cathba was a fair man. He gave orders to bring in the animals. His tone of voice suggested that the order was given merely to humour the four. How could bulls prove anything? While they waited for the animals to arrive, he did notice that Fiachart began to look extremely nervous.

A short time later, two slaves conducted the bulls into the presence of the waiting court. Last to enter was the Black Bull of Wisdom.

'Now prove your charges against Fiachart,' the Steward ordered.

Roisín called on Torc to step forward. When he did, she led him over to Cathba.

'This is the Black Bull of Wisdom, belonging to Maeve of the Thousand Spears,' she said. 'We were told to take him secretly to safety here, bringing two other black bulls to confuse any spy of Lú's who might follow us.'

She took the Steward's hand and placed it on Torc's horn. Then she questioned the bull about the events of their journey and their accusations against Fiachart. Amazement spread across the Steward's face as he heard in his mind the bull's voice, like summer breeze over rippling water, defending every claim the four had made. When all was revealed, he had Fiachart stand before him.

'Not only are you a false accuser,' the Steward told him,

'but you are yourself guilty of every crime you have accused these children of committing. In addition, you are Lú's spy, and in contact with his evil Anti-Druid, Archeld. You will be bound and imprisoned until I can decide on your punishment.'

Cathba directed the guards who had brought in the children to tie up Fiachart's hands and to conduct him out of the room.

The bulls were taken out to the meadow once more, where they were safe at last. The children went with them, talking to them and rubbing their foreheads affectionately. All four patted and stroked Lorc and Morc, who had travelled so humbly with them to conceal Torc's identity. *They* could not speak to humans as Torc could. Instead they rubbed their great heads against the children's shoulders, making gentle lowing sounds to show their pleasure.

'They love you,' Torc told the four, 'as I do. You were kind to us and took care of us, and brought us a long way, to a place where we will be safe.'

'We'll soon have to leave you,' Brona said, with tears in her eyes. They all felt sad at the thought of losing such patient companions after so long a journey.

Then attendants took the children to comfortable guestrooms, like those in Ardalba. They waited on them, brought them warm, scented water to bathe in, combed and perfumed their hair, and dressed them once again in the splendid clothes of High Nobles.

There followed an evening of feasting, music and storytelling which could not be matched outside the west. After it, the children slept in comfort and without worry, knowing the Black Bull of Wisdom had reached safe pastures where Lú would never find him. That part of their task was done. Next came the second part, which would take them all the way back to Ardalba to report to Queen Maeve on the bull's safe arrival.

13

Goodbye to Torc

Soon it was time for the four to leave the west, as Maeve was waiting to hear from them. The nearer the moment of departure, the sadder they all became at the thought of leaving Torc, Lorc and Morc. They knew they might never see them again. The evening before they left, they went down to the field where the bulls were resting after their long journey from Ardalba.

When Torc saw them, he trotted over, snorting and swishing his tail.

'We came to say goodbye,' Brona told him, 'and to thank you for all the ways you helped us and protected us.'

Together they put their hands on his horn to hear what he would say, and together they heard his voice whispering through their thoughts.

'You brought me safely here,' he said. 'I shall not forget you. You are still under Elk's protection, whether you meet him again or not, so no animal will hurt you. No person will hurt you either, now that I am no longer with you. This time you can enjoy your journey. Go safely.'

Each of the four in turn stroked the soft fur on his forehead. 'Goodbye, Torc,' they said. Each heard the bull reply, 'Goodbye, Aidan. Goodbye, Brona. Goodbye, Rory. Goodbye, Roisín.' They said goodbye to Lorc and Morc too before leaving the field. 'We'll miss you,' they said. 'We'll always remember you.'

They returned to the fort to prepare for the start of their journey the following day.

'You will not travel as slaves this time,' Cathba told them, 'but as the High Nobles you are. Your journey will be shorter. You will return directly to the silversmith's crannóg on Wild Deer Lake, travelling upriver from the Lake of Tranquil Swans. This way you will leave out the long trek back to Lord Datho's fort.'

Aidan reckoned the trip back would take less than half the time their outward journey had taken. They would travel with less hardship than when they had travelled as slaves.

The following morning, after dressing in the clothes of High Nobles, the four were ready to leave. Datho's steward and his household came out to see them on their way.

When the four stepped outside, they stopped short in surprise. There waiting for them were four strong white ponies, each held by its own groom. The ponies were bred from the wild stock that was found along the seaboard, and had not a single dark hair on their coats.

'Aren't they beautiful,' Brona whispered, going across to stroke the nearest one's nose, while he tossed his mane and nuzzled her hand with his soft lips. The others went to the other ponies, making friends with the animals who would take them home to Ardalba.

'The journey will be easier for you this time,' Cathba told them. 'I am lending my strongest ponies and four of my best attendants to escort you on your way. They will bring my ponies safely back when you have done with them.'

'We thank you for everything,' Aidan told him with feeling.

'We really do,' Rory added, and we hope the bulls will all like it here, and that you will keep them safe.'

As soon as he had spoken, a slave approached, leading the Black Bull from the pastures to bid a last goodbye. Again they held his horns so that he could speak to them all.

'Remember, Elk still protects you. Fear nothing,' he said.

'Goodbye, Torc,' they whispered, each rubbing his silky forehead and holding his horn for the last time. 'Say goodbye for us to Lorc and Morc.'

They mounted their ponies and rode away from the fort, an attendant leading each animal.

'Goodbye, Cathba,' they called. 'Goodbye.'

Cathba raised his arm in salute. The bodhrán player beat a slow march to his harper's strong chords while their ponies took them slowly away. The music continued until it faded into the distance and the Lord Steward and his people were almost out of sight.

'This is a better way to travel,' Brona said. 'Sandals on our feet, plenty of food with us, great ponies to carry us, and people to guide us.'

'You could say we are well attended,' Rory agreed. 'A groom for each pony, and four slaves to carry food and fire.'

'I feel safe this time,' Roisín added, 'now that we don't have the bull that seems to be wanted by everyone in the land. No one will mind us on our own.'

'We are safe until we meet up with robbers who want to steal our ponies, and perhaps our clothes and jewels as well.' This touch of reality from Aidan made them shiver in silence for a time.

Gradually they left the sea and cultivated lands behind them. The great Mountain of Sleeping Bears loomed high on their left, getting nearer by the hour.

'Will we stay for the night in the same cave?' Rory asked.

'Why not?' Brona answered. 'We were safe there the last time, and perhaps Elk will send the same bear to protect us again.'

'Do we need to go up as far as the cave this time?' Aidan wondered. 'Why not go straight across the Great Limestone Desert?'

'You've got a short memory,' Rory teased him. 'On the way out, Erla warned us to keep to higher ground, where there was shale and broken stone, and not to chance going over the flat limestone slabs, where we or the bulls could fall into dangerous fissures.'

Roisín agreed with Rory. 'We don't want the ponies to break their legs this time, do we?'

'Anyway, the cave is up there,' Brona reminded them all. 'I'd rather sleep in the cave than on this barren, open ground.'

Up and up they slowly climbed, the ponies' hooves slipping on the stones. When they reached the cave, the slaves who carried wood and fire made a campfire to cook a stew from food they had brought with them. The four thought it was better than the bread and cheese they had eaten on the way out.

During the night, while everyone was asleep, an enormous bear came to stand at the cave's entrance, where, unseen by anyone, he kept guard until dawn.

The next day they travelled down from the mountain in bright sunshine, and crossed once more the far edge of the

Great Limestone Desert. This time they stopped for a while at the Tombs of Ancient Kings.

'How ever did they build them?' Aidan wondered. 'They had no proper tools. Everything had to be shaped by hand, and carried or dragged by people. Yet there are dozens and dozens of tombs in this place.'

'There are an awful lot of dead kings. Where did they reign?' Roisín asked her attendant, Sorcha.

'Madam, they are kings from all the seven kingdoms of this land, buried here as far back as people can remember. The smallest tombs are the oldest. As time went on, men learned how to make them bigger and better.'

'They must be older than the Pyramids,' Rory thought, 'or at least as old as them.' He thought about shaping stone, a difficult enough task in modern times with power tools. How difficult it must have been for Stone Age people!

Leaving the tombs, still moving down the slopes into woods that crowded around the mountain base, they came near to the place where Erla had left them to return to Dara Mor. Before they knew it, they were once again in sight of the river along whose banks wolves had threatened them, and which they had crossed on giant stepping stones.

'Should we camp here?' Aidan wondered. 'Perhaps we will find Elk again. We must thank him and say goodbye to him properly.'

'It's more likely that he will find us,' Roisín said, 'like he did the last time.'

No wolves howled that night as the slaves prepared their meal and set up camp. When darkness fell the sky was cloudless and full of stars. They had never in their lives seen stars shine so intensely.

'Aren't they brilliant?' Brona said. 'I never saw so many.'

'That's because in this era there are no street lights or lights from nearby towns to dim the stars and hide the fainter ones.' Roisín had always loved watching stars and planets. 'And you're staring right up at the Milky Way, at billions of stars all together.'

Each of the four lay gazing upwards, knowing they would never forget this sight, until their eyes closed and, one by one, they slept.

While their slaves and grooms got ready to move on the next day, the four took a short walk to look for Elk, but found no sign of him.

'I would like to meet him again.' Brona sounded lonely.

'We all would,' Rory told her, 'but he comes and goes as he pleases. No one can summon him.'

At the last moment, when they were turning from the river to mount their ponies, they saw Elk standing as before, where the river bank sloped up to higher ground.

At once their ponies knelt before the lordly king of animals, as the bulls had done. The children walked up to him, unafraid, in spite of his huge antlers. Rory stroked Elk's velvet forehead. 'Goodbye, Elk,' he said. 'Thank you for taking care of us.'

Each of them in turn rubbed Elk's forehead and thanked him. 'We'll never meet you again.' Brona's voice was sad. She knew they would not remain long in the Kingdom of Ardalba after they had reported back to Maeve.

Elk's musical voice addressed them for the last time. 'Who can see future events, or know surely that we will never meet again? Goodbye, all of you.'

With that he turned from them and strode majestically

away into the distance. They watched him until they could see him no more.

They mounted their ponies and the attendants led them on again. All day they travelled towards the Lake of Tranquil Swans on Shining River, knowing they would reach it before nightfall. They looked forward to their journey upriver to Wild Deer Lake, where the silversmith had his crannóg. They could hardly wait to meet him again.

14

The Lake of Tranquil Swans

While they had been speaking with Elk, their grooms and attendants had waited down by the river. Now Aidan's groom came to make a suggestion.

'We are here by Shining Water, Master, and will soon cross it at Clochán Steps. Would you like to continue from there by boat, up the river to the Lake of Tranquil Swans, and then upriver again to Wild Deer Lake, where Samhain's crannóg stands?'

The four looked at each other. Why had they not thought to ask if that was possible?

'Where would we get a boat?' Roisín voiced the first problem that occurred to her.

'What would we do with our ponies?' Rory had grown fond of his.

Aidan's groom smiled. 'I have a friend near here who would lend his boat, and who would travel with you if you wished. We ourselves would bring the ponies to meet with you further up. They and the boat would make the same speed, I am sure.'

'Let's do it, then,' Rory said. 'I love boats.'

'It would save you the long and tiring land journey,' the

groom told them, 'and the lake is beautiful at this time of year.'

Brona waited to hear what the others decided, afraid that she would influence them by showing how excited she was at the prospect of the boat trip. She gave a squeal of delight when it became clear that travelling on by boat was their unanimous choice.

Before long, they reached the bridge of giant stepping stones, which they had crossed on their outward journey. Mighty men of the Stone Age had moved these giant boulders to their present resting place, and not even Shining Water could carry them away.

After they had crossed Clochán Steps, Aidan's groom left them and went to fetch his friend, Fachtna. The groom soon returned with a stocky, smiling, fair-haired man, whose skin was weathered brown by wind and sun, and whose smile revealed a gap where a front tooth was missing. At once the four knew they would like Fachtna.

'I can bring you to Samhain's crannóg,' he promised, 'but it will take more than one day to get there. Rowing against the flow of water is a slow business. My second oarsman and I will grow tired and will need rest. Perhaps in the evening we might come ashore and meet up with your attendants, who will see to your needs.'

The four thought this was a good arrangement. They travelled on to Fachtna's village, where he showed them his boat. It was bigger than Samhain's coracle, and had been made from the hollowed-out trunk of a massive oak.

'That's a great boat,' Rory said, and Fachtna bowed with pride, accepting the compliment.

'My father is the head of this village,' he told them. 'He

and I made the craft together. It is the best boat on the river, from Wild Deer Lake to the sea.'

Later, after they had eaten, the village harpist began to sing songs of great deeds of the past, when all men had the strength and bravery of heroes and all women outmatched them in power and beauty. The villagers took part by clapping and giving shouts of approval, their faces glowing darkly in the light of the fire they sat around. The four knew they would sleep soundly that night.

In the morning, Fachtna had his boat ready. Aidan suggested that they should bring two of their attendants to help with the rowing. That would give Fachtna and his friend Cumal some time to rest, and there would be no need to stop the journey except during darkness.

Soon all was ready for the long river voyage. The grooms and ponies prepared to set off to follow the river upstream, keeping the boat in sight as much as they could. The entire village came to cheer them on their way.

That day the weather was glorious. The gentle breeze of their passage kept them cool even in the noonday heat. They watched the morning mist lift to reveal distant mountains, purple with heather, that formed a backdrop to the vivid green of surrounding meadows and woodland.

'This is *OK*,' Rory said emphatically. 'I can stand this.'

'It seems too easy.' Roisín sounded worried. 'Remember how hard this journey was for us when we went the other way? Why did Datho not think of sending us by boat?'

'We had three bulls with us,' Brona reminded her. 'Could you imagine three bulls on this boat, big as it is?'

Aidan laughed. The idea of even one bull seemed ridiculous, never mind three. 'We managed all right on land,' he said. 'Bulls were not made for this sort of travel.'

Steadily the oarsmen pulled on their oars, before leaning forward to bring them back for another stroke, scattering droplets of water, like diamonds in the sunshine, when the oars broke the surface. Boat-length by boat-length, the river bank slipped past them as they inched their way upstream. Then, before they realised it, the banks slipped further away. The river grew wider. Its strong current became less noticeable.

'Now we are coming to the Lake of Tranquil Swans,' Fachtna told them. 'This is one of the best parts of the journey.'

That evening they landed at the lakeside to meet the rest of their party. The ponies were glad to see them. Their attendants made camp, ready for the night. As darkness fell, they all sat around the fire, singing and telling tales. It was a fitting end to a great day.

Fachtna woke them at first light the next morning. His boat was waiting for them, curtained in mist. They set out on the lake, disappearing into white cloud that swirled about magically, sometimes thinning out so that they thought they could see distant shapes moving ahead of them, sometimes deepening until they could hardly see each other.

'This is like fairyland,' Brona said. 'You could believe you were invisible.'

Later the rising sun grew stronger and the mist crept away. They could enjoy the passing scenery again. They noticed salmon in the water, and herons on the bank. In one place they saw small deer coming to the lakeshore to drink.

The sun rose higher in the sky. Following it from the

eastern horizon, to their right, came dark clouds. Sooner than anyone realised it, clouds had covered the sun, casting a cold shadow. A chill breeze sprang up. Clouds overhead stacked into thunderheads. Before they knew it, a storm was on them.

Lightning flashed again and again. One peal of thunder followed another. The bitter wind strengthened, whipping the surface of the lake into rough water. Large waves threatened the boat continuously, white water breaking around them.

'Sit still!' Fachtna shouted. 'Hold on to something. We should soon be out of this.'

They were not soon out of it. Their craft was helpless, Fachtna unable to steer it against wild gusts of wind that buffeted it in every direction. The four held to their seats, fearing they would be thrown out of the rearing boat, fearing that the boat itself would overturn in icy squalls.

Then Aidan shouted, 'Look ahead! I see something. Is it land?'

Dark cliffs loomed suddenly in front of them, half-hidden by the spray of waters striking against them. Fachtna and Cumal struggled with all their strength to keep the boat off the rocks at the base of the cliffs. Inch by inch they drifted past crags that spelt death to anyone trapped on them. As the boat worked its way around the cliffs, the rocks were replaced by a gravel beach. Everyone on board helped to bring the boat towards the shore, and they waited until the water finally lifted them up with the next wave to carry them well inshore. When they crashed down on the rough foreshore, Fachtna felt the rowlocks splinter and knew that his boat was badly damaged – it would go no further without repair.

Wet and miserable, the four fought their way up the beach against the gale. They huddled together under the protection of a large rock, until Fachtna and Cumal had drawn the boat up to safety, and came to join them.

'This is an island!' Fachtna shouted over the storm. 'It's in the middle of the lake. We'll stay here until morning, when I can begin to repair the broken rowlocks. We can't use the oars without them.'

The four realised they would get no supper that night. They settled into the driest spot they could find to wait for sunrise. High winds sang their own lullaby and the four fell asleep in spite of themselves.

15

Ulcas Spellbinder

The sound of hammering woke them. Fachtna was using his axe to shape new rowlocks from an oak plank. It looked like hard work.

'Can you fix it?' Rory asked. 'Can I help? I'm good with jobs like that.'

'Thank you, Noble Rory,' Fachtna replied. 'It may well be that your skills surpass mine, but my father and I decided long ago that no one except he and I would ever touch this boat to repair or alter it. We want every part of it to be ours alone. Can you understand that?'

'That's all right,' Rory told him. 'I know how you feel. I don't like people tampering with things I make either.'

'Give me until the sun is overhead,' Fachtna said. 'The new rowlocks will be at least good enough by then to take the oars and get us off the island. In the meantime, I'm afraid our food has been damaged by water. Look around. See what you and your attendants can find.'

They left Fachtna to his work and set off in search of food. When they had left the beach far behind them, they saw they were once again in woodland. They rummaged around for fruits and edible mushrooms, while their attendants set snares for squirrels. Before long they could no longer see the lake, and the sound of Fachtna working had faded away. It was quiet under the trees, except for the rustling of small animals through fallen leaves, or the muted cries of birds. It seemed to become quieter with every step they took. Aidan, who was out in front, suddenly held up his hand to warn them. They crept up to where he stood and looked in the direction he was pointing. Outside a tiny circular hut sat the oldest man any of them had ever seen. He was dressed in black animal skins and his black hair fell down in untidy tangles round his shoulders. His face was brown and wizened, like a walnut. He stared at a pot that hung simmering over a charcoal fire in front of him, and muttered a sing-song chant.

'Let's go back,' Roisín whispered. 'I don't like the look of him.'

They turned to go, but a stick caught Rory's foot and he lost his balance. The old man looked up sharply at the sound.

'And who be ye?' His voice sounded like a hinge in need of oil – a squeaky, rusty sound. 'Who be ye, sent to spy on me and learn my secrets?'

'The storm blew us to this island,' Aidan told him. 'We don't mean any harm. We're not spying for anybody.'

'By mighty Archeld,' he replied, ' I shall prevent harm. I am Ulcas Spellbinder, apprentice of Lord Lú's great Anti-Druid. Stay where you are until I have finished my work here. Then I will deal with you.'

The four stood rooted to the ground, afraid to move, while this ancient, malevolent person continued to chant over his simmering pot. Brona was standing behind the others. She thought Ulcas had not seen her yet. Slowly she began to back away, step by step, so quietly that the other three did not hear her. Soon there was some distance between her and the old man's hut, and she could walk more boldly. She wondered if he had noticed there were four of them. What could he do to them? It was enough for Brona that he had mentioned Archeld, evil Anti-Druid of Lú.

When she was far enough away, she climbed up into a tree, from where she could still see the others. They were standing in front of the old spellbinder, whose chant became louder and louder, though they did not know what language he used. Then he got up, still chanting, and began to pace around the fire, going faster and faster as he got louder, until he could go no faster and chant no louder. When he stopped abruptly, silence descended on the forest once more.

'That's that spell finished,' he gloated. 'Archeld will be pleased. This potion will make his enemies shrink until they become invisible and can harm him no more.'

He turned then to the children. 'No one who has seen me work my spells can escape to tell the tale. I am going to place you under the spell of forgetfulness, so that you will believe you have always been my slaves, and will remember no other existence.'

'We're leaving now!' Aidan shouted. 'Come on,' he called to the others.

Brona, watching from her tree, wondered why they did not run away, why Aidan himself seemed rooted to the spot.

'Ha!' Ulcas snorted. 'I have already put a binding spell on you so that you cannot move. You didn't see me do that, did you?' His small, evil eyes leered at them triumphantly.

Brona realised that she had escaped in the nick of time, before Ulcas noticed there were four of them. Rory, Aidan and Roisín looked helplessly at each other. They were so frightened by now that they didn't realise that Brona was not with them. They thought she still stood behind them. Ulcas gave an evil laugh. He walked over to them and began his spell, chanting in a strange language as he had before and waving a branch of the rowan tree over each of their heads in turn. Before Brona's eyes, small blue tornados seemed to sweep around each of her friends, faster and faster, in time with Ulcas' chant. When the chanting ceased, they suddenly stopped, leaving the three standing with downcast faces before the Anti-Druid's pupil.

'Get about your work,' he snarled at them. 'Clean my hut. Fetch fresh water. Prepare my supper.'

In despair, Brona saw the three move off like zombies to do Ulcas' bidding. When he went back to his fire and his spells, she took a roundabout path to follow Rory, who had gone to fetch water. Down by the lake, she thought she would be safe enough from the threat of Ulcas. She ran up to Rory and pulled him down to crouch beside some bushes.

'Rory, let's go for help,' she said. 'We can save the others too.'

Rory looked at her with dull eyes. 'Who are you?' he asked in slurred tones. 'Who are these others you speak of?' He tore his arm away from her and turned back to his work, without interest or curiosity.

Brona realised sadly that the spell of forgetfulness had worked on Rory and the others. It was up to her alone now to rescue them all from the power of Ulcas. She knew the first thing she had to do was to stay well away from Ulcas himself, so that he could not put *her* under any evil spell.

'What else can I do?' she asked herself. 'I cannot look

into my moonstone without help. And who is there to help me now?'

Brona wandered off among the trees. She felt suddenly hungry and stopped to look for food. When she had eaten some wild berries and nuts she felt heavy sleep coming over her. She looked for a safe nook between two tall trees and, hoping there were no bears on the island, she closed her eyes and gave in to this strange and sudden tiredness.

Much later Brona began to waken up. She heard leaves rustling close to where she lay. She opened her eyes slowly, being careful not to move in case danger was waiting. But there was no danger, only a giant badger snuffling around in the undergrowth. All of a sudden, Brona felt lonely. When the badger moved within reach of her hand, she stretched out her fingers to stroke the pure white band on his head. As soon as her fingers came into contact with the badger, Brona heard his voice as she had heard the voice of the Bull of Wisdom and King Elk. He spoke in quiet sighs of breath. Brona had to listen carefully to catch his words.

'Oh Noble One, welcome to my kingdom,' he said. 'I am Forest King of this island. Who are you? And why are you troubled? It may be that I can help you.'

Brona was glad to have found a friend. She told the badger everything about the shipwreck, and how it happened that they had come under the power of Ulcas. She described how Ulcas had put Aidan, Roisín and Rory under a terrible spell of forgetfulness, and how she was left alone to help them.

'I *could* help them,' she told Badger, 'if I could only use the power of my moonstone to speak with Scathach, Queen Maeve's Arch-Druidess. But I need someone who can look into the stone while I concentrate, to enable me to use the second sight it gives. I cannot do it by myself.'

'I can do that for you.' Brona thought she saw a smile on the badger's face. 'I have the same powers as the Black Bull of Wisdom and King Elk. People do not know that because I live quietly on this island, but it is true. Now I will use my power to help you.'

So in that quiet corner of the forest, Brona held her ring up for Badger to see. He rested his head on Brona's knees and gazed into the moonstone's misty depths.

'Close your eyes now,' he told her. 'Calm your thoughts. See only the stone with your inner eye, leaving all else aside. Look in the depths where colours glint. Follow them to the stone's heart.'

Brona held the stone with its iridescent tints in her mind's eye, until in its secret depths she saw Scathach standing before her, her face darkly shadowed by her midnight-blue cloak, the emerald snake eyes of her jewelled druidic staff flashing green sparks of twinkling light.

Brona saluted the great Arch-Druidess. She told her of their shipwreck in the storm, and how Ulcas Spellbinder had put Aidan, Roisín and Rory under a spell of forgetfulness.

'This is a strong spell,' Scathach told her, 'a spell that few have confidence enough to break. It is not too strong for *my* authority, though. I shall help you to release your friends from it.'

'Thank you, great Scathach,' Brona replied. 'I shall do all you tell me.'

'This is what you must do,' Scathach said, 'and you must do it while Ulcas is somewhere else and cannot see you.

Seek a hazel twig with three leaves on it. This will be your rod of power. Find your friends while they sleep. Walk to your left in a circle around them. As you go, use your hazel branch to scratch a ring around them on the ground at your feet. When this ring is complete, step inside it. Command the sleepers in your loudest voice, "Scathach bids you wake." I will watch you with my own power of second sight, and at that moment I will lift the spell. Your friends will wake up with full memory, as before.'

Before Brona could thank her, Scathach faded from her view. She opened her eyes to the island woodland, and Badger waiting in front of her. 'Come on, Badger,' she said. 'Let's find the others. I know what to do now.'

They travelled back towards Ulcas' hut, making no noise in case he should hear them. By the time they got near it, darkness was deepening over the island.

'I will be your eyes,' Badger told Brona. 'I am a creature of the night. I can see in the dark. Ulcas must not find you.'

Leaving Brona to rest against a tree trunk, Badger went forwards, snuffling around the hut and beyond it, looking for the three bewitched children, until at last he found them. They were huddled together on some straw, sleeping the sleep of forgetfulness. Badger hurried back to fetch Brona.

'Where do I find a hazel twig?' she asked him. 'We can't go without that.'

'Look on the ground for hazelnuts,' he told her.

Both of them went searching beneath the trees around them. It was Brona who first found old hazelnut shells on the ground. She reached up to the lower branches of the hazel tree that stood above them, and pulled off a long twig with three leaves. Then, walking carefully so that she would make no noise, she followed where Badger led her, around the hut of Ulcas, to where her friends slept on their bed of straw.

There she followed the instructions of Scathach. When she had completed the ring on the ground, right around the sleeping children, she stepped into it. She hoped Ulcas would not hear her shout when she called to them.

'Scathach bids you wake,' she commanded them in her loudest tones, and she felt the power of the Druidess flowing through her. At once the three were awake, their forgetfulness lifted from them.

Badger looked uneasy. 'No one outside the circle could hear you shout,' he told Brona, 'but perhaps Ulcas sensed it when his potent spell was broken. Follow me quickly now. I will take you to the far side of this island, where Ulcas never goes.'

Without hesitation, they followed Badger until they reached a small beach, with a handy cave nearby where they could hide.

'You are safe now,' Badger told them. 'Ulcas does not come to the lake on this side of the island.'

It was time for Badger to go. They all said goodbye to him and thanked him for his help. Brona had grown so fond of him that she wished she could take him back with them. She stroked his white stripe one last time before he left. They watched him slip back into the bushes.

'We have to find Fachtna and Cumal.' Aidan said what they were all thinking.

'Let's stay by the shore and go around to where we landed,' Rory suggested. 'Fachtna will surely have finished his new rowlock by now. You can go in front, Aidan, because you're so good at finding your way everywhere.'

So Aidan led them, keeping the water's edge in sight.

It was almost morning when the four rounded a curve in the shoreline and saw Fachtna's boat pulled up from the water's edge. They knew they were safe. They could always trust Aidan's orienteering experience to find the way back for them from wherever they had been. Fachtna was delighted to see them.

'I thought harm might have befallen you,' he said, 'but I see now that you have been quite safe.' The four looked at each other and said nothing about Ulcas or the danger they had been in. 'My boat is fixed again,' Fachtna told them. 'We can travel on now.'

Roisín had been considering their situation since she had woken from the sleep of forgetfulness. She feared other dangers might be waiting for them on the lake.

'Could you bring us across the lake to where we could meet our grooms again?' she asked Fachtna. 'It's been a lovely trip on the river, but I think we would rather go on now by land.'

Aidan, Brona and Rory looked at her in amazement. Each of them had been thinking exactly the same thing. It proved again to each of them how close they were to each other.

'We've really enjoyed the journey,' they told the boatman, 'but it would be good to reach dry land again.'

'Fair-weather sailors, that's what you are,' Fachtna said, laughing. 'Of course. I'll bring you to where your attendants are waiting. In any case, you are almost at Shining Water again. It will be a short land journey up to Wild Deer Lake and Samhain's crannóg.'

Leaving the island, Fachtna directed his boat towards

the western shore, where in the distance the lake began to narrow to a point, at which it once again became a river. They soon saw their horses and attendants waiting for them at a stretch of sandy shore. Fachtna landed them there expertly.

'Goodbye,' they called to him. 'Have a safe journey.' Fachtna and Cumal waved goodbye, then rowed away, back down the lake. The four watched them until they were out of sight.

The children at once mounted their ponies and their attendants led them forward again. All day they travelled up Shining River towards Wild Deer Lake, knowing they would reach it before nightfall. They looked forward to meeting the silversmith again and spending the night at his crannóg.

16

Back to Samhain

It was late evening before they saw lake waters ahead of them, and the distant dwellings of the fisherfolk. They were thrilled when they recognised where they were. They could hardly wait for the welcome and the feasting Samhain would give them.

'He thought we were slaves,' Roisín reminded them. 'He won't expect High Nobles. Maybe he won't recognise us.'

'He wouldn't be a master craftsman unless his eye could take in detail,' Aidan answered. 'He'll recognise us all right.'

'He might ask us about Fiachart.' Brona had a grin from ear to ear.

'If he does, *I'll* be delighted to inform him how Lú's champion ended up.' Rory knew he had a tale to tell. He couldn't wait.

They came to the village near the crannóg, to where they had first met Merle. Across the lake, lazy smoke was rising from the roof opening of Samhain's sturdy dwelling. They looked for Merle among the women who were with the children in the shallows, but did not see her. The chief fisherman, when he heard of their arrival, came to greet them, bowing before them to ask what their pleasure was.

He did not know them from their last visit, not having expected the slaves he had met earlier to be the centre of such a rich travelling party now.

'We wish to visit the crannóg,' Aidan told him. 'We shall wait for the coracle,' he added, remembering the last time. At that, Aidan's attendant, who had often travelled to visit Samhain with Lord Datho himself, blew a special call on his horn. It was the call used to let Samhain know that his overlord, Datho, wished him to send his coracle to the village to fetch him across.

'But it's only us,' Brona giggled when the attendant told her what he was doing. 'Samhain will be angry when he finds out it is not Lord Datho.'

'Indirectly, you do come from Lord Datho,' the attendant replied. 'You have the right to use his call.'

This time it was not Samhain but his son Cormac who brought the coracle. As before, attendants and rowers accompanied him, and they chanted the same chant while they crossed the water.

Cormac was a big man, like his father. An attendant carried his spear upright in the boat, and held his heavy shield, made of wood covered with animal hide. Cormac held his sword with its point down on the slats in the bottom of the boat, the jewelled hilt clasped in his huge hands. He wore heavy rings on both hands. His thick cloak of brown homespun, fastened with an ornate pin at his shoulder, was heavily embroidered round its hem. Its hood hid his dark, handsome face.

Cormac was not angry to find it was not really Datho who had summoned the coracle. He was delighted to meet his friends again, but he looked so pale and sad they knew at once that something dreadful had happened.

'Samhain went hunting by himself yesterday morning,' Cormac told them. 'He prefers to follow deer on his own. He has not returned since. The fisherfolk and ourselves searched all day.'

'That's awful,' Brona whispered. 'What could have happened to him?'

'Either he has had an accident, or wild animals have injured him, or an enemy has captured him.' Cormac sounded exhausted.

'I suppose Lú has other spies around besides Fiachart.' Rory spoke slowly. 'Why would they attack the silversmith?'

'I don't know,' Cormac said. 'Will you wait a few minutes while I go with the head of the fisherfolk to get some fish from him? I won't be long. Then we'll go back to the crannóg.'

The fisherfolk all trailed away after their overlord's son. The children and their attendants were left to themselves.

'Will we take a walk?' Brona suggested. 'They'll be gone for a while.'

The others knew she was up to something, and Roisín asked the grooms to look after the ponies so that the four of them could walk off and be on their own. They left the river bank and walked back among the trees until they were out of sight and sound of the village.

'What? What is it?' they all asked Brona.

'Well,' she said, half-grinning at the thought of her plan, 'we still have our moonstones. Do you think we could use them to find out where Samhain is, even though we don't have the bull to help us? Could we try them ourselves?'

Roisín, Aidan and Rory thought this was a great plan.

Each of them was sorry that they had not thought of it themselves. Brona made them go further into the woods, where they would be sure no one could see what they were doing.

Brona decided that they would work in two pairs, in an effort to increase the energy flowing through the stone. She and Rory would seek the message, with Aidan and Roisín channelling it, as the bull had done for them before, and as they had seen Scathach do for Queen Maeve.

'You'll have to lend me your ring, Aidan,' she said. 'I used mine on the island and there hasn't been a full moon since.'

Aidan took off his ring and handed it to Brona. 'You stand nearer to the other world than I do,' he said. 'You will get a clearer message.'

Brona and Rory sat on a fallen tree trunk, their feet resting on green moss. Roisín stood in front of Brona and Aidan in front of Rory. Brona and Rory held up their moonstones in their right hands, so that Aidan and Roisín could look straight at them. Roisín put her right hand on Brona's shoulder, and Aidan put his on Rory's.

Looking intently at Rory's moonstone, Aidan spoke to Rory and Brona as he remembered Scathach doing. 'In your mind see only the moonstone, nothing else. See only the stone. Keep your mind empty. Let the stone fill it. See the changing colours at its depth. See nothing, but only the stone.'

Brona and Rory gently closed their eyes and slowed their breathing, concentrating on visualising the stone. Aidan and Roisín continued to stare intently at the moonstones in their rings.

'What can you see?' Roisín demanded. 'What does the stone show you?'

Brona and Rory answered together in slow, dreamy tones. 'I see the forest where we went hunting with Samhain. I see bare hillside beyond. A boar surprises Samhain while he watches for deer among the trees. He is knocked over by the boar's charge. Now he is up again. He lances the boar with his spear but does not kill him. The boar retreats among the trees. Samhain travels up the hill to where he knows there is a cave to shelter him for the night. He finds the cave he seeks, but the wounded boar follows him and traps him there. Then the boar charges Samhain and gores him.'

They stopped. Their eyes remained closed.

'What else can you see? Can you find the cave?' Aidan sounded frantic at the thought of the danger Samhain was in.

Again Brona and Rory answered together. 'We know where the cave is. It is a day's journey from here. Samhain lies there, his leg gored by the tusk of the enraged boar. He has lost much blood. He is weak and cannot help himself.'

Aidan took his eyes off the moonstone then, and so did Roisín. The others opened their eyes as if they were waking from a deep sleep. They all looked at each other, big grins spreading over their faces.

'We did it!' they shouted. 'All by ourselves we looked through the moonstone.'

'Now we have to take Cormac to Samhain,' Brona said. 'No bed for us tonight.'

17

Saving Samhain

When Cormac returned with his fish, the four were waiting for him in great excitement.

'We can take you to your father,' Brona told him. 'We know where he is.'

Cormac looked at her in puzzlement and doubt. 'You know where my father is? Why didn't you say so before?'

'We didn't know before,' Roisín assured him. 'We found out just now, while you were getting the fish.'

'You couldn't have,' Cormac said. 'You weren't speaking to anyone.'

'Weren't we?' Aidan challenged him. 'We are now High Nobles of Maeve of the Thousand Spears. We have special powers. We used our power to learn where Samhain is.'

'Let's go,' Rory insisted. 'Samhain is wounded. His life depends on how quickly we find him. Instruct your people to bring a litter to carry him home.'

Once convinced that they knew how to find his father, Cormac wasted no time. He organised a search party made up of his own people and the fisherfolk. He sent two back to the crannóg to fetch weapons and food. He arranged for torches and people to carry them. He brought warm bearskins and lengths of coppice wood, intending to use them to form a stretcher. As soon as everyone was ready, they set off. The children were glad to have their ponies. They felt they would have collapsed from tiredness if they had had to walk any further, after travelling all day long.

This time Rory and Brona led the way. They were the ones who had seen the woods and the strange hillside through the moonstone. They were confident they would recognise landmarks, though they were in countryside they had never journeyed through before. Lit now by flares and torches held aloft by the fisherfolk, the forest looked menacing, dangerous and darker than dark. The searchers moved in silence for the most part, overawed by the night.

'I hope we are still protected by Elk,' Aidan whispered to Roisín. 'This place must be full of wildlife, from bears to squirrels.'

On and on everybody plodded, for hour after hour, men who had already searched for most of the previous day now almost asleep on their feet. The ponies, too, were weary, as were the children. They had already covered many miles since morning. Yet Samhain was hurt and in danger. No one wanted to delay.

Stumbling through darkness and the ghostly shadows cast by fisherfolk's flares, they covered many miles, until they saw the sky lighten as dawn arrived in the east. At last, with this first light, Cormac called a halt for food and a brief rest. He looked doubtfully at Rory and Brona.

'Are you two sure you know where you're taking us?' he asked.

'Of course we do,' Brona told him. 'We are going to Samhain by the quickest route.'

'We'll soon be out of these woods,' Rory consoled him. 'It will be easier then.'

When all had eaten, Cormac got the search party on the move again. In another hour they had got through the forest, as Rory had promised. The ground rose before them, first through meadowland, then through thinning vegetation and heather. Soon they were at the foot of a bare mountain, all shale and stones, its summit still hidden, shrouded in morning mist.

Brona pointed upwards. 'Samhain is up there,' she said. 'We'll reach him before noon.'

With this encouragement the party began to climb. When they pushed up the steep mountainside, their feet dislodged loose stones that tumbled behind them down the incline onto those who followed. The ponies began to slip on shingle that moved beneath their hooves. The children decided they would walk without them the rest of the way, leaving them in the care of one of Cathba's grooms.

By now the sun was fully risen. Everyone felt its warmth, welcome at first after the chill of night in the forest, but it was soon to prove too hot for people exposed to it without shade, people who were climbing as fast as they could in the attempt to reach Samhain and bring help to him before it was too late.

Cormac tried to imagine Samhain on the mountain. Where could he go if danger threatened? Nothing grew here. Nothing provided shelter. He could see no hiding place.

In spite of Cormac's doubts, Brona and Rory continued on without hesitation.

'We're looking for a sort of overhang with a cave entrance under it,' Rory told Cormac. 'It's not far from here, so get everyone to keep a lookout for it.'

Up and up they went in the hot sun. They all peered ahead, searching the barren hillside, shielding their eyes from the sun's bright glare. Suddenly Cormac gave a shout. 'Look!' He pointed ahead. 'There's a crag with what could be a cave-opening beneath it.'

'You're right!' Brona and Rory spoke together. 'That's the place we're looking for.'

'Maybe it is,' Cormac said, 'but is my father there? Will we find Samhain?'

Rory and Brona climbed more quickly now that their goal was in sight. They knew Samhain would be in poor shape after the boar's attack. They hoped they would be in time. Cormac stayed by their side. The rest of his party hurried to keep up with them.

Soon they could see that there was indeed a cave-opening in the rock ahead of them. Cormac and his attendants began to call his father's name. Their loud cries of 'Samhain! Samhain!' echoed thinly over the hillside. When they paused to listen, they heard no response, only the stillness of this remote place.

At last they got to the cave's mouth. Brona and Rory stood back to allow Cormac to enter before them. They and the others followed close behind him.

Like the Cave of Sleeping Bears, this cave had a relatively narrow entrance that widened out to a large chamber. Light from the opening shone into this space. There, at its far end, they found Samhain.

He was badly wounded, his right thigh gored and bloody. His forearms too were bleeding and raw. He watched them approach, but his weakness was so great that he could not speak.

Almost at his feet lay the body of the largest boar they had ever seen, impaled through the heart by Samhain's hunting spear. The boar's eyes were open like Samhain's. They stared the fixed stare of death.

Cormac saw that it had been a mortal struggle, in which Samhain and the boar had equal chances. He was in awe at his father's bravery and strength, to have prevailed single-handed against such a fierce animal, which would normally need several hunters to trap and kill it. Yet Samhain, already badly wounded, had done it alone.

'Make the litter,' Cormac instructed his attendants, 'and bring food and water,'

While this was being done, he folded his own cloak to use as a pillow beneath Samhain's head.

Roisín, well trained in first aid, looked at the wounded warrior. His teeth chattered and he trembled with cold and shock, in spite of the fever that drenched his forehead with perspiration. She wiped his face gently with the hem of her cloak. 'He needs to be kept warm,' she told Cormac. 'He is shivering.'

Several attendants offered their travel cloaks to wrap around the stricken man. Roisín soaked some bread in water to soften it, and put it to his lips. Samhain did his best to eat it, but weakness and weariness undermined his efforts. He turned his face away, and Roisín urged him no more.

In a short while the litter was ready. Cormac directed attendants to lift his father gently on to its bearskins, and at the same time to keep him wrapped as closely as possible in warm cloaks. He ordered two other attendants to hang the boar's body on a spare length of the coppice wood they had brought to make the stretcher, and to carry it back with them to the crannóg, so that all there might see the fierce size of Samhain's attacker, acknowledge the Master's strength and bravery, and realise how it was that he had been wounded so badly that he was almost at death's door.

Everyone was now ready for the march home.

'You'll have to halt for rest at short intervals,' Aidan told Cormac, after speaking with Roisín. 'Samhain will get shaken up, no matter how carefully they carry the stretcher. He will need to lie quietly for a while now and then, to recover his strength.'

'Surely the quicker we get him to the crannóg, the better,' Cormac said with a frown.

'There is a stream further down the mountain, before we enter the woods. Let that be our first stop. Roisín can do a lot to help him,' Aidan said.

Cormac could see for himself how ill his father was. Grudgingly he agreed to what Aidan suggested. 'But if this stop does not help him, we stop no more,' he decided.

They all had to travel at the pace set by the litter-bearers, who moved carefully down the slope of the mountain so as not to jolt their master. The slow procession eventually reached the stream Aidan had mentioned. The bearers laid the litter gently down by the water. Samhain closed his eyes in exhaustion, wrenched and shaken in spite of his bearers' concern.

Roisín instructed the attendant who carried fire to get some timber blazing. She ordered water to be carried from the stream and boiled over the fire. She tore up Brona's linen cloak and her own to make washcloths and bandages. When all was ready, she set about preparing Samhain for the long trek home.

She bathed away the blood on Samhain's thigh where the boar had gored into muscle, and checked that the severe bleeding had stopped. She examined his forearms, which were now swollen and bruised. They were covered with defence wounds, caused by his attempts to shield himself from the boar's attack. She cleaned his face and his dry, cracked lips. Then she applied bandages to the puncture wounds made by the animal's tusks penetrating his legs, and to his forearms, which bore marks of the boar's teeth. She hoped that no infection would follow. Samhain's violent shivers had now stopped. She kept him well wrapped still, and had the litter moved as near to the fire as was safe.

Meanwhile, Brona had sent people to look for birds' eggs, and to see if there were trout in the stream. One man found two pigeon's eggs. Others caught four small trout. Brona boiled the eggs. An attendant stuck a gutted trout on a stick and held it over the fire to cook it. When this food was ready, the two girls fed Samhain with their fingers, off plates made of leaves. Slowly and with growing energy, Samhain ate what was offered. Then, to everyone's delight, he found enough strength to speak to Cormac.

'I was stalking deer down in the wood when by chance I disturbed the boar,' he told his son in a laboured whisper. 'He attacked me, but did me no harm. I wounded him there among the trees, though not enough to kill him or stop him running away. Later, when I had reached the cave and prepared to spend the night there, he followed me and cornered me in it, goring and biting me. I am lucky to be alive.'

That effort drained Samhain's energy. He closed his eyes in exhausted sleep. His attendants picked up his litter to carry him home. Cormac walked beside it, watching his father with worried eyes.

After the food and his short rest, Samhain's vigour increased with every moment that passed. Later in the day, having eaten again, he decided he no longer needed the litter, the heavy weight of which his attendants had borne so willingly. Not yet strong enough for a long march, he accepted gladly when Aidan offered him the use of his pony.

They brought the silversmith back to the village. All his people came out to welcome him, rejoicing in his safety. Later his coracle took him to his crannóg, rapid beating of the bodhrán proclaiming to all that the Master was safe and was coming home.

The children were honoured by all of Samhain's people. Cormac told everyone how he had searched for his father in vain until Rory and Brona had used their special powers to lead him to the cave. Samhain added his own thanks. 'They saved my life,' the silversmith said. 'I would not have survived another day without help.'

He gave orders for them to be made comfortable, as well as for feasting and games in their honour. For three days there were contests, sports and music, with storytelling and merriment. Samhain's harpist sang of their great deeds, composing as he sang. The four realised they would go down in local tradition as heroes.

On their last visit to the crannóg, they had been treated as slaves, waiting on others and eating only when everyone else was satisfied. This time they had seats of honour, and took part in everything as the High Nobles they were.

Then came the morning of their departure. They had grown even fonder of Samhain and his son, Cormac, now that they could talk to them as equals rather than as slaves to their masters. They were sorry to leave the crannóg and the friends they had made there.

'If you hadn't taken us to Datho in the first place, we would never have got there safely, or found our way to him at all,' Roisín told Samhain. 'We were completely lost. We shall always remember your kindness to people you thought were slaves.'

'Nothing could repay you for saving my life,' Samhain replied, 'but to thank you, I am sending two of my best warriors to escort you to Ardalba and defend you against danger on the way. They will wear the amber cloaks of Datho's fort to show that their overlord and mine is Datho himself. No one will attack a party protected by the powerful Lord of the East.'

They all thanked him. Rory spoke for all of them. 'We will never see you again, but we shall never forget you.'

Samhain shook their hands in the local way, grasping them by the forearms. 'Who knows what is in our future?' he said. 'Can we say surely that something will never happen again?'

They were taken off the crannóg to the bodhrán's beat and the song of rowers, and all Samhain's people came out to bid them farewell. On land, the fisherfolk waited to see them off. Their grooms and attendants stood with their ponies prepared, and with all they would need for a pleasant journey.

Samhain gave them his final gift at that moment, before getting back into his coracle to return to the crannóg. 'My men carry a silver platter, made for a monarch, for you to present to Maeve of the Thousand Spears. It will express my gratitude for what you, her High Nobles, have done for me.'

It was sad to leave the silversmith. Slowly they mounted their ponies and turned their backs on Wild Deer Lake and Shining River. They headed towards Maeve's kingdom. In the distance they soon saw the mountain that looked like a sleeping dog with a long back. The peak showed the shape of its head. They knew that far on the other side, Maeve waited to hear of the safety of her Black Bull of Wisdom.

18

Ardalba and Home

The journey from the crannóg back to Ardalba was their best yet. They had grooms, attendant slaves, and Samhain's warriors to smooth their way. Their grooms led the ponies. The warriors caught small animals to add variety to their food. They no longer had to worry whether they were going the right way, because everyone else knew exactly which was the most direct route. They had warm bearskins to sleep on and no worries about spies following them.

Before they knew it, they were on the other side of Sleeping Dog Mountain, and could see Maeve's mighty stronghold ahead of them. It was like a homecoming.

Lookouts from Ardalba saw them while they were still a great way off. Many High Nobles came out to meet them and escort them on the last steps of their long journey. The children felt at home again on seeing the colourfully embroidered white cloaks of Maeve's palace guards.

Chief among the Nobles who came to greet them was Magdawna, who was delighted to have them back. 'My mother has followed your way,' he told them. 'She has known that you and her Black Bull of Wisdom were safe. She and Scathach consulted the stone.'

As soon as they reached the palace, they were brought into Maeve's presence.

'How did you fare?' she asked them warmly. 'And how is my bull? Come, sit by me here and tell me how you met the many dangers on your way.'

She put them sitting in one of the deep window seats that were let into the thickness of the palace wall. Servants placed Maeve's own cushioned chair of carved oak so that she could sit among them to hear their tale.

They told her the whole story of danger and excitement, interrupting each other so that no detail was lost. They assured her that the bull was safe at last with Datho's steward on his pastures by the Western Sea. They spoke of Datho's help, and of Samhain's. They recounted Fiachart's treachery, and his kidnapping of Rory. They mentioned King Elk, who had protected them from any hurt while they were in his kingdom. When they had finished, Maeve spoke.

'No Nobles have ever served me better. When Lú heard that the Black Bull of Wisdom was no longer in my kingdom, he turned north to go home with his army. In saving the bull, you have saved all of us, particularly my son Magdawna. He is our champion and would have been first to face Lú in combat, and perhaps would have met his death. We of Ardalba thank you. As ruler, I wish to honour you by naming you "Rescuers of the Realm". I will do that before the feast begins tonight, when all will be present to witness it.'

All the High Nobles rejoiced with Maeve of the Thousand Spears at the children's success in bringing her bull to a secure haven where Lú could not find him, so saving Ardalba from conflict.

Then Samhain's warriors brought the precious silver

platter, which their master had sent in grateful recognition of what the four had done to save his life. The children presented this to Ardalba's queen.

Later, when the palace had grown quiet again, they went to their rooms to prepare themselves for the great honour they were to receive. They told their attendants that they needed to be dressed for an important occasion, and their attendants did not let them down. Rory and Aidan had their hair brushed and dressed as nicely as its short length allowed, and on their foreheads the attendants placed gold bands which encircled their heads. Their tunics were the usual soft, finely woven white linen, reaching to their calves and held at the waist with finely tooled leather belts. This was to be a ceremonial occasion, so their tunics had heavily embroidered collars, and the hems were gold-fringed. Over the tunics, each wore an elaborate sleeveless jacket. Aidan's was midnight-blue, Rory's scarlet, and both had gold clasps instead of buttons. As a mark of the honour to be given them, each wore a full-length white cloak. They felt proud to wear Ardalba's own colour. It made them feel that they belonged in this strange place and among these people. On their feet they wore sandals bound with gold.

Brona and Roisín were not idle either. Roisín's rich chestnut hair was dressed and oiled until it looked burnished. Her attendant then selected six sections of it, each one to be elaborately plaited and adorned with golden beads. These plaits dropped down among the rest of her hair, which fell loosely in shimmering waves. Brona's hair was too short for this treatment. It was brushed and waved and allowed to fall naturally, after her attendants had tied many river pearls into it. They shone out of its blackness like stars from dark skies.

Both girls had full-length gowns and cloaks. Brona wore a violet cloak over a pale green dress, both of which were enriched with silver clasps and brooches, to complement the pearls in her hair. Roisín's cloak was orange, over a dress the colour of primroses. Both colours set her chestnut hair off perfectly. Her gold jewellery contained many amber stones that went with her clothes.

No sooner were they ready than a messenger came from Maeve to summon them to the great hall, where she was holding court. They went down together. When they walked through the door, they saw all the High Nobles waiting at their places for them to arrive. They walked in and across the room, to where Maeve of the Thousand Spears stood to receive them, while a great shouting, cheering and clapping burst from the assembled company, who all rose to their feet to honour the children who had done so much, and undergone so much, for Ardalba.

They stood in front of Maeve, as they had done on the day of their arrival. She raised her hand for silence, and waited for the cheering to stop. Then, when she could be heard in every corner of the hall, Maeve spoke.

'It is not often noted in our annals,' she began, 'that we name an individual "Rescuer of the Realm". It has *never* been noted that we named four at once. Today, that is what I do. On your behalf and on behalf of Ardalba, I now declare Aidan, Rory, Brona and Roisín to be Rescuers of the Realm. They have earned this as individuals and as a group.'

Maeve signalled to an attendant to draw near. He carried a cushion with four sashes laid out on it. Attendants placed cushions in front of the children so that they could kneel. Maeve lifted the ornamental sashes one by one and put them over the heads of the four children, placing them on their right shoulder and letting them fall diagonally across their chests. Each sash had an embroidered gold emblem to signify that they were Rescuers of the Realm.

'Now,' she said, 'you will go down in our annals as Rescuers of the Realm.' She turned to her annalist, Ogma, who stood by. 'See to it,' she ordered

And there, before the whole court, the four watched their names go onto Ogma's stone tablets and knew they were now part of Ardalban history.

This time all of them spoke together. 'Thank you, Majesty, we are deeply privileged.' That was the signal for another outburst of cheering from the gathering.

When quietness returned to the great hall, Scathach slipped from where she stood in a far corner, and came over to the children.

'I commend you,' she said. 'You are truly High Nobles of this land.'

Brona took her hand to thank her for her help since their arrival. 'Without you, Arch-Druidess,' she said, 'we might still be under Ulcas' spell.'

'And without you, Brona, I could not have broken it.' Scathach smiled at her, then turned to the other three. 'Of all of you, Brona is most like myself. She is truly a Druid in the making.' Then she took her leave of them and left the hall.

That evening, long feasting began in honour of Aidan, Roisín, Brona and Rory. There was more dancing and music, more song and storytelling. For three days it continued. Would it ever end?

In the middle of all the rejoicing, the four children

thought again of home and their parents. They decided that Brona should be the one to speak to Maeve about their longing to return to Glenelk. Seizing a moment when they found the queen alone with her dogs, walking outside the fort, Brona bowed deeply to her. 'Majesty, we have lingered a long time at Ardalba. Soon we must return to our own time and place, and to our own people.'

Hearing this, all good humour left Maeve's face.

'You wish to leave?' Her voice was high-pitched with disbelief. 'Ardalba is not good enough for you? We have not honoured you sufficiently?'

'We have parents and friends,' Brona told her. 'We miss them.'

'You are people of destiny,' Maeve declared fiercely. 'You have been sent from a distant time and place to save Ardalba in times of distress. I cannot allow you to go. Speak of it no more.'

With that, she marched back into the fort, her dogs following her.

Later Roisín called the others together where they could talk and no one could hear them. 'She won't let us go willingly.'

'How can we get away, then?' Brona asked. 'There are guards all over the place.'

'Best to go in broad daylight,' Aidan suggested. 'The guards are most careless after the midday meal.'

'What would Maeve do if she caught us?' No one answered Brona's question, while they thought about it.

'How do we know she would do anything to us? She might just let us go,' Rory said.

'No, Rory, she wouldn't do that.' Roisín sounded certain. 'She thinks we are powerful people, with magic from a future age. She'll find another task for us.'

'Roisín's right,' Aidan said. 'If we want to return to where we belong, we have to do it without Maeve knowing.'

'We can't go back looking like peacocks.' Brona pointed to her High Noble's clothing. 'We need camouflage. Have we still got the slaves' clothes?'

'Yes, we have,' Rory replied. 'Cathba's people put them in our packs, on the ponies he lent us. Mine are now in the chest in my room. So are my real clothes.'

Real clothes! Real clothes meant Glenelk and home, and their parents. They all suddenly realised what in fact they had been in danger of forgetting – they didn't really belong at Ardalba at all.

'Right then.' Brona started planning because she liked to be prepared for everything. 'After the midday meal today, we go off to our rooms as if to rest. We don't go in a bunch. We just drift off quietly, one by one. We put on our real clothes, and then put the slaves' clothes over them. If we pull the cloaks down, they should hide our jeans. No one will get close enough to see us properly, I hope. Are we agreed about all this?'

'We agree all right, but how do we get out through the stockade?' Aidan asked. 'They always guard it, don't they?'

'We went out through the small back gate the last time,' Roisín reminded them. 'Do they ever have guards on that?'

'We can try it anyway. They won't look too closely at slaves.' Rory felt excited at the adventure they would have in escaping. It seemed more real to him than any dangers they had met with in their journey with the bull.

After the midday feasting was over and everyone, including the guards, had slaked their thirst with Maeve's good mead, the children slipped off one by one to their rooms. Their jeans and anoraks seemed strange to them after such a long time in other garments. They put their slave clothes over them, turning up their jeans and making sure that their cloaks were worn so as to cover everything else.

The palace had grown quiet and its people were resting. The four crept out the way Alton had first brought them without meeting anyone who would stop them. There were no guards at the small back gate. They went quietly through it. They were outside the fort's defences now, but could still be seen should anyone look out. They circled carefully around the stockade towards the front of the fort, keeping close to trees and bushes whenever they could. Soon they could see across the narrow valley to the small hill where the cave was, through which they had first entered Ardalba.

They crept along under cover as much as possible. When they crossed open ground, they went in ones and twos, so that no one would see four people together. They went as slaves might – not hurrying, but not delaying.

When they were far enough from Ardalba not to be seen from there, they stayed together and moved more quickly. Before long they were climbing the hill up to the bank, where they began to look for the small entrance to their cave. They knew overgrowing bushes would hide it, because they had had to struggle out through bushes into Ardalba when they had first arrived there.

Suddenly, across the valley they heard a distant commotion. Bodhráns beat quick tattoos, horns blew to summon guards, dogs barked.

'They've missed us.' Brona went white.

'Maybe,' Aidan agreed, 'but does that mean they know where we are?'

'Come on,' Rory urged, 'keep looking for the cave. Spread out a bit.'

'If they're using dogs they might soon know where we are,' Roisín responded to Aidan. 'We did tell Maeve where we had come from.'

Each one of them searched frantically. Knowing the cave entrance had been well hidden when they left it, they had to make sure that they looked behind every growing thing. Meanwhile they could hear Maeve's searchers getting closer. Soon they could see them at the bottom of the slope. It was only a matter of time until someone looked up and saw the four of them.

At last Rory called urgently from further along the bank. 'I've found it. Come here quickly. We don't want them to follow us into the twenty-first century, do we?'

One by one they slipped through the tiny opening. Aidan, who was last in, shook out the branches they had disturbed, so that they hid the cave completely once again. When they were all inside the cave, they could no longer hear Maeve's search party.

The cave passage seemed darker than ever after the bright sunshine outside. This time they had no torch. Brona was not sure where she had lost it. They all knew they could not go wrong, even in darkness, because there was only one tunnel to follow. It would lead them back to the Valley of Rocks. Each of the four kept one hand on the wall as they moved forward, and the other on the person in front of them.

Step by step they inched along, until they came to the first turning.

'The next bit is much longer,' Rory remembered. 'I didn't like it.'

'This is what pitch dark means.' Brona's voice sounded muffled as she led them through. 'You have to go by feel.'

'We'll get there,' Aidan said. 'There are no side turnings for us to get lost in.'

'Look!' Roisín sounded cheerful. 'You can see a bit of light ahead now.'

And so they could. Dull, grey light, still far away, but a lot better than pitch blackness. It got stronger as they moved towards it.

Soon they were at the second bend in the tunnel, where they had to squeeze through the narrow turn they all remembered. Now the light was much stronger, though there was still not enough to light their way. On they went, one foot in front of the other, until they came to the opening into the inner cave. It seemed a lifetime since they had explored that for the first time. Across the centre of it lay a beam of light from the outer cave leading to the Valley of Rocks.

'Maybe we should change our clothes here,' Roisín suggested. 'We can't go back to Glenelk in slaves' cloaks.'

'Good idea,' Aidan agreed. 'We can hide the slave clothes in this cave. No one at all seems to come here.'

Each of them took off their slaves' clothes. They brushed off their own clothes that they wore underneath. They rolled down their jeans, and took their shoes and socks out of their sacks. Soon they looked as they had the day they explored the cave. They searched for a place to leave their

Ardalba garments, then stacked them in the darkest corner. Rolled up inside them, they left their High Nobles' moonstone rings.

'We can't take any of this home. I hope it will be safe here.' Rory sounded sad to have to leave everything there. 'I hope nobody finds it. I liked the moonstone ring.'

Dressed again in their everyday clothes, they climbed through the small opening into the main cave. Here they sat in a circle where the light was strongest.

'Are we going to tell people in Glenelk about Ardalba?' Aidan asked. 'Would it be a good idea?'

They thought back to their adventures there, to people they had met, magic they had witnessed and taken part in, animals whose strange powers had helped them. Brona thought especially about the badger, King of the Island, and of Lorc and Morc, the two gentle giants who had travelled so bravely with Torc, to keep him safe. And they thought of their code of honour as High Nobles, trusted not to harm Maeve's kingdom.

'I say we tell no one.' Brona spoke first.

'I agree. No one would believe us if we did tell them.' Roisín made her feelings clear.

'We must say nothing,' Rory said. 'People might try to reach Ardalba themselves, and that would not be fair to Maeve or to her other High Nobles.'

'I'm glad we all think that way,' Aidan said. 'As High Nobles, we undertook to be loyal to Ardalba. Let it be our secret.'

'We are *still* High Nobles,' Brona reminded them, '*and* Rescuers of the Realm. We must be loyal to each other, even here in Glenelk.'

'Come on then, let's go,' Aidan said, when they were ready.

They climbed out through the small opening into the main cave, walked across it, and wriggled out into the open air. To their relief, they were back in the Valley of Rocks.

'Thank goodness.' Brona spoke for all of them. 'Glenelk is still here.'

'What time is it?' Aidan wondered.

Roisín and Rory took their watches out of the pockets of their jeans, where they had hidden them.

'It's only five o'clock,' Roisín told them. 'That's about the time it would have been if we'd never gone to Ardalba.'

'And it's the right date,' Rory added. 'My watch shows dates.'

'We'll be home for tea.' Brona felt she could do with some modern food again, like fish fingers or pizza. 'Queen Maeve was right about time. We came back here through the exact same passages that took us to Ardalba, and time here has stood still, waiting for our return.'

On they walked through the Valley of Rocks and along the road to town. There was their school and the church, just where they had left them. To their relief, the church clock agreed with their own watches. They really would be home for tea.

When they got back to the Town Hall where they usually split up to go home, they looked at each other and grinned.

'Guess what?' Rory said. 'We've been in another time and place, and our parents won't even have missed us. Would you believe that?'

The four of them laughed and turned to go their separate ways. Each of them felt that Ardalba had changed them. They knew its influence would never leave them.